A NOTE FROM THE GRAVE

Welcome to the first issue of Living Dead Press Presents, a magazine dedicated to not only horror, but the behind the scenes of the horror community. This is the first of what (for now) will be a two issue run. Why not more you ask? Simple. Making a magazine is a lot of work, and I mean a lot of work. Writing a book is child's play compared to what it takes to make a magazine. The formatting alone is so time consuming, well, there's a reason why there aren't more horror magazines out there. So if you're thinking, "If it's so damn hard, then why did we here at LDP bother?" That's simple, too, because we wanted to say we did it, that we did something most small presses wouldn't even attempt, and not only that, but we did it damn well.

So, knowing we were only going to do a few issues, we wanted to make sure they were packed full of cool stuff, such as interviews with horror writers, movie and book reviews, cool artists with artwork that should blow your mind, and other horror tidbits any horror fan should enjoy. And as we are a book company foremost, we made sure to add a healthy dose of horror fiction, as well. So even if you don't want to read the articles, there's enough horror stories in this magazine to fill a small anthology all on its own. This is an amalgam of a magazine and a book, something no one has done before in the horror world. Sure, there are horror anthologies and sure there are horror magazines, but not the way we've done it, by blending the two and doing it all in blood-splattering color! So if anyone ever says it can't be done in the world of the small press, I say send them our way, because if there's one thing LDP has proven over the past two years since it's creation, is that:

1.) We don't do things the way everyone else does, and,

2.) We don't know what the word no is. Hell, we'll try anything once, just to say we tried. So I hope you enjoy this magazine as much as my staff and I enjoyed making it, and remember, what you hold in your hands shouldn't exist. But in the world of Living Dead Press, what shouldn't exist often does.

Editor Anthony Giangregorio

EDITOR: ANTHONY GIANGREGORIO

FORMATTER: JESUS "DARK RIDDLE" MORALES

CONTRIBUTING WRITERS

REBECCA BESSER
JOHN SKERCHOCK
JIM BRONYAUR
JESSICA A. WEISS
MATT NORD
KEVIN MILLIKIN
DARREN GALLAGHER
JASON ANDREW
TONY SCHAAB
DANE T. HATCHELL
DAVID H. DONAGHE
KEVIN JAMES BREAUX
RICK MOORE
ALAN SPENCER
KELLY HASHWAY
ADAM P. LEWIS
GRANT WAMACK
JOE FILIPPONE
JOSHUA RAMEY-RENK
KEIRNAN KELLY

SPECIAL THANKS TO:

JOE MCKINNEY,
ERIC S. BROWN,
ARGYLE GOOLSBY AND
GARY MCLUSKEY

Table of Contents

ISBN Softcover ISBN 13: 978-1-935458-97-5 ISBN 10: 1-935458-97-3

For more info on obtaining additional copies of this magazine, contact:
www.livingdeadpress.com

MONSTERS 101: The Origins of a Phenomenon By John Skerchock

Welcome to the first of what I hope are many articles detailing the history of the horror genre as we know it today. You see, there is a reason you decided to read this magazine. Perhaps it was because you're curious about a genre you are unfamiliar with? Perhaps it's because you've been a long time fan of monsters, whether in literature or film, and wanted to add this magazine to your collection? Being a fan and participant of a hobby is fun, but do you know its origins? I've been involved in this genre most of my life. For those of you who don't know me, that's almost fifty years! I've grown up in this genre, and I know many of the people who are responsible for making it what it is today, and I want to tell you about them and more. You see, horror is a genre deep within the realm of fantasy which also includes science fiction. Horror can cross those meager boundaries and exploit them to create some wonderful entertainment. Fantasy is a genre within romance because at one time novels like Frankenstein and Dracula were seen as romances. In this article, I will talk about movies and books, horror personalities, actors, horror show hosts and even toys. You have to know from whence you came, and I think I am the creature who can tell you. Right now I want to talk about the origins of modern fandom, or Monstermania, as it has been described. It's time to turn the clock back to the 1950s. That's where it all began. Television was in its infancy and Baby Boomers, those born between 1946 and 1965, were the first to really experience this new technology. And certain forces in the atmosphere were congealing to create something special. At this time several things were coming into play to create what could be described as a monster boom a few years later. First, a television station in New York ran a marathon of the original KING KONG for twenty-four hours straight. People were ecstatic. Many hadn't seen this movie since its first release decades before, and children were becoming hypnotized by this awesome monster and those Hollywood visual effects. Universal Studios saw television as a way of re-airing many of its old films. Folks at the studio bundled up all those old horror movies—FRANKENSTEIN, DRACULA, THE WOLFMAN, THE MUMMY—into a package called Shock Theatre, and peddled the package to television stations across the country. This package of films came with a book detailing each movie and listing ways in which the movies can be shown to benefit the wallets of the TV stations. One suggestion was that the station should create a host to introduce the films. This host, or emcee, became known as a horror host. Many TV stations took this advice and horror hosts began popping up on TV screens all across the country. Their job was to create an atmosphere for the viewers. Most hosts donned scary makeup and played up the movies with little adventures of their own during commercial breaks. Most often these performances were done live and very little film exists of their antics today. The target audience for these films was the adult market because they were meant to be shown late at night when children were asleep and all regular programming was done for the day. But somehow the children found out, stayed up late, and watched while hiding behind chairs and sofas so that Moms and Dads wouldn't find them out of bed. In the meantime a company in France, in 1957, published a one-shot magazine featuring all kinds of stills from classic horror movies. The magazine became a sensation and received publicity in American magazines. This phenomenon caught the attention of James Warren, a Philadelphia native with an urge to make money. Warren decided to publish his own one-shot and make some fast cash. He located a science fiction fan by the name of Forrest (Forry) J. Ackerman who had recently been featured in Life Magazine because of his huge collection of movie stills and memorabilia, and enlisted his aid. Forry provided stills and information and Jim put it all together to create Famous Monsters of Filmland. This magazine was so odd and unusual that

distributors didn't know how to market it and newsstand owners didn't know where to place it among their other titles. Yet, it became a hit. The magazine sold more issues than expected. Kids discovered it and loved it. Warren had created a 'monster' and was amazed. Suddenly the one-shot was to become a regular series. Warren had no idea how long the popularity would last, but it was one wave he intended to ride until the end. Also during this time, a young film company in England was making a gory splash. Hammer Films began their rise to power first with a few black and white science fiction hits but then with full color blood and gore recreations of DRACULA and FRANKENSTEIN. New monster faces of Christopher Lee and Peter Cushing became familiar icons along with Boris Karloff, Bela Lugosi, and Lon Chaney to millions of kids across the country. And here in the USA, a shrewd promoter was doing his best to keep that horror wave rolling: William Castle. Castle not only created some of the spookiest movies of the time with A HOUSE ON HAUNTED HILL and THE TINGLER, but he played up his movies by going to cities and promoting them in regular spook show fashion. Spook Shows were created in the 1930s and survived into the 1960s, and they're seeing a revival right now. A Spook Show is a monster movie, usually a matinee, with a horror host, often a magician, who entertains the audience, brought in other 'live' monsters and offered prizes that led into the feature movie.

     This was a big deal for children who flocked to these shows. All of this was going on within a one year period. It was a tidal wave of monsters coming at people from all different directions. And it was only going to get better. Some of the horror hosts could sing. Tarantula Ghoul put out a record. Zacherley, known as Roland in Philadelphia but he changed his name to Zacherley when he moved to New York, was a friend of Dick Clark's and had a hit single with 'Dinner With Drac' and an album called Zacherley's Monster Mash. Zacherley put out a number of albums over the course of three years and they have been recently collected and released on CDs. (Zacherley has had several CDs of new material put out recently but we'll spend more time with Zacherley in a future article.) The Aurora Model Company decided to ride the wave by releasing a series of six plastic monster model kits. These kits were so popular that a second series was produced. Kids growing up during this period had a challenge. This was before cable television when most homes only got three channels—if they were lucky. Many hours were spent pouring over the TV Guide, looking for monster movies. If you were lucky you got to see your favorite monster movie once a year, but most kids saw them once every two years. By the mid-1960s some homes had cable television but that meant you only got thirteen channels and you still had to hunt for the monster movies. Television studios were riding the wave by producing The Munsters, Bewitched, and The Addams Family. In fact, a 1964 issue of Life Magazine called 1964 the Year of the Monster. Remco, Ideal, MPC, Palmer, Transogram, and other toy companies began producing monster toys. You could drink out of monster-themed glasses by Anchor Hocking or take a bath with monster-themed soap products. More monster products were planned but then one night in 1966 it all came to a sudden halt. Color television was brand new. Only the year before, the networks decided that almost all new shows would be filmed in color. And Batman starring Adam West and Burt Ward debuted. Monsters were quickly forgotten as kids turned to this new craze: superheroes. It didn't all end there. Of course monster television shows were cancelled, and a lot of stations got tired of rerunning old monster movies week after week. The movie studios still made monster movies. Hammer was at its best through this decade, and Famous Monsters was still going strong, surrounded now by imitators of all sorts. Warren had expanded his magazine base with monster magazines featuring all comics: Creepy and Eerie. Vampirella was soon to follow. A hold out to the cancellations was a soap opera known as Dark Shadows. It started as a gothic series but it couldn't get an audience. In a last ditch effort to save the show, the writers threw in a vampire and the series suddenly did an about face. Its popularity grew but it was a single phenomenon. Other networks tried to introduce supernatural soap operas but they failed. And Dark Shadows failed in the long run shutting down in 1970. The series was brought back in 1991 with Ben Cross as Barnabas Collins but the series failed. Perhaps Johnny Depp will do better in the Tim Burton film which begins shooting in spring of 2011? Many of the kids affected by this first monster boom carried within them a love of monsters that went with them the rest of their lives. They were called Monster Kids. This term was coined by USA newspaper editor David Colton as he described the Baby Boomers that were brought up by horror hosts as their baby sitters and monster toys in their toy boxes. But by 1966 it wasn't cool to like monsters anymore so the die hard fans had to go underground and love their monsters in secret. A reprieve came in 1970. By this time The Munsters and The Addams Family were seen daily in reruns along with classic shows like The Twilight Zone and The Outer Limits. Kids were getting ready to experience monsters again. Independent TV stations were again offering monster movies on Saturdays. Some even re-introduced horror hosts like Philadelphia's Dr. Shock and New York City's The Creep. Aurora models brought back their monster model kits in new boxes with glow-in-the-dark pieces. Famous Monsters was thriving. Its catalog of monster-themed products called Captain Company assured that fans had available to them the latest and greatest in monster-related merchandise. DC Comics was having a huge success with its horror titles—House of Mystery, House of Secrets, The Witching Hour—thanks to wonderful artwork by Bernie Wrightson and Neal Adams. Famous Monsters Magazine held two monster related conventions in 1974 and 1975 in New York. Fans were gathering and forming friendships. It was a great time to be a Monster Kid. But again the boom, which lasted longer this time, came to an end. Science fiction became the rage with the release of STAR WARS in 1977. A year earlier a new magazine hit the stands called Starlog. It offered glossy pages and color pictures of science fiction movies. And the TV networks began to offer science fiction as part of their programming. Monsters were again becoming a thing of the past. But they didn't go quietly into that good night. The monster fans retaliated with FRIDAY THE 13th, HALLOWEEN, and zombies. The next decade or so wasn't a good one for fans of classic horror and monster movies. Unable to compete with the new direction, Famous Monsters folded as Jim Warren walked away from his company. Fans will tell you that the last few issues weren't the best as the magazine tried to compete by offering more science fiction but the lack of color pictures sealed its fate. Famous Monsters ended some ten issues short of 200 in 1983. Starlog spawned Future and other science fiction magazines popped up. Yet monster movies were fighting back. They were creepier and gorier as blood and guts spilled from the screen. Special effects master Tom Savini rose to fame during this time with his gruesome work on DAWN OF THE DEAD (we'll see more of Tom in a future article). And Fangoria Magazine was born. Throughout the 1980s, monster movies became kill factories as teens were torn to shreds by Freddy Krueger, Jason, and Michael Myers, zombies, psychos, and crazies. A special magazine was created to focus just on this bloodshed called Gorezone.

    Horror Hosts still made an appearance now and again with Commander USA on the USA Network showing old monster movies, Stella on SATURDAY NIGHT DEAD in Philadelphia showing monster movies, and Morgus, syndicated to major cities like New York still reached out to us. An attempt was made to bring back a classic monster magazine with Forry Ackerman at its helm, but after three issues it failed. It looked like monsters were a thing of the past. But there was something isle that kept the flames of monster fandom alive, and that was video tape. In 1984, video recording machines became affordable and so did the movies to watch in them. People began creating home libraries of monster movies to keep their interest alive. Now they could watch monster movies anytime and not have to hunt for them amid all the trash that was on television. By the end of the 1980s, something was stirring in the universe. The Monster Kids, those Baby Boomers weaned on monsters, were now adults and beginning to show themselves as fans of classic monster movies. In Illinois, Dennis Druktenis founded Scary Monsters Magazine in 1990, and in New York, Kevin Clement created Chiller Theatre and held its first monster convention in a school gymnasium. And there were others. They came out of the darkness with their monsters: beautiful resin kits hand-sculpted to perfection with loads of detail. Aurora and other classic monster kits were being re-introduced in resin format, and movie stills and press kits from thousands of horror movies were suddenly on the marketplace. Then a man named Ray Ferry had had an awesome idea. If historians had to point at one thing that created the current monster craze, it would probably be the 1993 Famous Monsters Convention in Virginia. This convention was created by Ray Ferry who had formed a friendship with Forry Ackerman. The intent was to judge the strength of monster fandom to determine if it was feasible to resurrect Famous Monsters Magazine. This show pulled out all the stops. Dealers in monster merchandise came from all over the world. Hollywood movie props were on display. Every horror personality still alive was there. It was an incredible event, and at its closing an announcement was made that Famous Monsters would return.
This convention was followed by a major Dark Shadows convention in New York and a horror convention in Pittsburgh called the Zombie Jamboree, featuring stars of the zombie movies filmed in that area. And England held a major convention of Hammer Horror stars. The time was right! This time fans had the aid of the Internet. They could stay in touch with each other and support each other. It was easier to be a monster fan because you knew of other people like you who shared the same hobby. It was no longer considered childish to discuss your favorite monster movie openly. Fans wanted more, and they got it. FANEX was a horror-themed convention in Maryland. Fans could go to Chiller Theatre in the spring and fall and then FANEX in the summer. Then came the Monster Bash convention in western Pennsylvania. Fangoria began having conventions. Other horror conventions popped up across the country and are still around today like Cinema Wasteland, Horrorfind, and Monstermania. By the end of the 1990s monsters ruled again as was evident when the U.S. Postal Service released the classic monsters postage stamps featuring Boris Karloff, Bela Lugosi, and Lon Chaney. Universal Studios licensing of monster-related items was at an all time high. Sideshow Collectibles came out with a series of eight and twelve inch articulated monster figures with accessories. Amok Time and other companies joined in and monsters were everywhere. Polar Lights, a new model company, brought back the original Aurora monster models and fans bought them up. In fact, most of the monster collectibles that you'll see on Ebay today are from these wonderful times. Today fans are now connected through the Internet and it's more acceptable to say you like monster movies than it was thirty years ago. Monsters aren't just for children unless you consider that we really are children deep down inside. Monster shows are held everywhere. Famous Monsters is back for a third time after a dispute between Forry Ackerman and Ray Ferry brought the title to a sudden end and in bankruptcy only to be bought by a young entrepreneur. Scary Monsters Magazine, Monsters From the Vault, Screem, Fangoria (the only magazine to survive from the Starlog family), Scream (from England), Horrorhound, and other magazines flourished, and monster toys are still being created. Websites featuring monsters and horror hosts abound. Moebius Models is the new company resurrecting old monster models while adding a few new surprises.
Most monster movies are available on DVD or for download and make watching horror films so much easier. Gone are the days when we had to search every inch of the TV Guide to find out when a horror movie was being aired. When only three channels existed this was a necessity. Cable made seeing monster movies more frequent, but there is nothing better than owning them and having your own Spook Show. It all sounds pretty good, but you need to know this. As a monster fan you are still in a minority. If you go to a Universal Studios store and ask where the monster souvenirs are, you'll be told that monsters don't sell. Most people have no interest in collecting monster-related items. The premiere monster website is www.universalmonsterarmy.com. It's a club of sorts where you can meet other monster fans, see wonderful pictures of monster toys from the 1950s to present, and spend time making new friends. But the site only has just over 2000 members. That's not a lot for a worldwide site when you consider that the Star Wars chapter covering Pennsylvania, Delaware and Maryland has over 100,000 members! There you have it. It's brief but that's where the current fandom comes from.

John Skerchock is the author of four books related to horror. He's had more than a dozen horror stories published. He is a columnist for Scary Monsters magazine but has also written for Horror Biz, Castle of Frankenstein, Chiller Theatre, and Screem magazine to name a few. He also does book reviews for www.zacherley.com.

AN INTERVIEW WITH JOE MCKINNEY

LDP: Please tell us a little bit about yourself and how you came to be a writer.

JM: I still don't think of myself as a writer, even though I've been doing this gig professionally since 2005. I've been a San Antonio police officer for nearly 15 years now, and I still think of that as my primary job—despite the fact that the writing pays better. Writing was always just a hobby for me, something I did whenever the mood came over me. Growing up, I'd write the occasional short story, staple the pages together, proudly put them on the corner of my desk, and then promptly forget about them. There's no telling how many short stories I threw away over the years. But then I became a dad, and that experience changed me on a fundamental level. Suddenly, the world seemed very complicated, I was supposed to be a grown up, and I started looking for ways to define my place in the world. Writing seemed the natural way to do that, so I sat down to write a novel. Dead City was the result. And, as luck would have it, the book sold well enough that I was able to turn an occasional hobby into a full time, paying gig.

LDP: What are the titles of your books?

JM: I've written quite a few over the last few years. My first novel, Dead City, has turned into a franchise called the Dead World, and now encompasses the novels, Dead City, Apocalypse of the Dead, Flesh Eaters and The Zombie King. I've also done a stand alone non-zombie horror novel called Quarantined; a crime novel called Dodging Bullets; a short story collection called Nightmares and Grimoires; and edited two horror anthologies, one about zombies, called Dead Set, with Michelle McCrary, and another on abandoned buildings, called The Forsaken, with Mark Onspaugh. I have six more books, all horror novels, coming out over the next two years.

LDP: What are your books about?

JM: I'm known for zombies, but I write in quite a few genres, such as crime fiction, science fiction, true crime, horror, even culinary history and anthropology. But I think the most conspicuous element of my fiction is a strong emphasis on police procedure. It's something I know a lot about, and it forms a strong current in my storytelling.

LDP: What do you think people would like about your books and why?

JM: Based on the letters I've received from readers, people seem to respond to the cinematic quality of my writing.

My writing process is to rehearse a scene over and over again in my head before I start writing, and I think that translates into a reading experience in which it's very easy to get absorbed.

LDP: What inspires you as a writer?

JM: Most stories, regardless of genre, can be seen as some version of the guardian/ward relationship, where one character has some degree of responsibility for the welfare of another. They either do this job well or poorly, depending on the current of the story. This is true of my stuff, certainly. For me, that inspiration comes from my role as a father. That's what makes me a man, and that has given me the emotional grist for my writing mill.

LDP: Who's your favorite writer?

JM: Wow, that's a hard one. I'm reminded of the saying, "There are two types of horror writers working today—those who were influenced by Stephen King, and those who are lying when they say they weren't influenced by Stephen King." He influenced me, certainly, and continues to do so. But he's not my favorite. I think if I had to pick just one writer for that distinction, it would be Charles Dickens.

Of course, ask me again tomorrow and I might tell you something different.

LDP: What's your favorite genre to read?

JM: I love reading history, but only when they focus on very narrow topics. Broad, sweeping histories tend to be frustratingly vague. But biographies, or books that look at a large scale event through the point of view of a specific person, practice or organization, make for fascinating reading. One recent example was a history of Russia's transition from a Czarist state to a Communist one as experienced through the eyes of the Smirnoff Vodka Corporation. Stuff like that fascinates me.

LDP: What's your favorite genre to write?

JM: Oh, that's easy. Horror all the way.

LDP: What advice do you have for writers?

JM: If you want to be a professional writer, behave like a professional. Think of this as a job because that's exactly what it is. Show up to work everyday. Be on time. Get to know the business. Turn out a consistently high quality work product. You get the idea. Be a pro if you want to get treated like one. But I can give you one great tip nobody seems to practice anymore. Never ever underestimate the power of a handwritten thank you note. It'll move mountains for you.

LDP: Of all the characters in your stories, which is your favorite and why?

JM: Stephen King once remarked that for every writer, every good writer, there comes a story that pushes their comfort zone way beyond what they thought they were capable of doing. For me, that story was my novel Quarantined. It was the first time I'd attempted a book length narrative through the point of view of a female character, and to get that right, I really had to focus on my craft. That experience did more to push me as a writer than anything I'd done before, and for that reason, Lily Harris, the main character of Quarantined, is my favorite.

LDP: Have you ever co-written anything with another author? If so, was it a pleasant experience?

JM: I co-wrote a novel called Lost Girl of the Lake with Michael McCarty, and yeah, it was a great experience. Sharing a creative project with another writer can be frustrating, because you have to give up some measure of control, but it can also lead to some amazing chemistry, as it did with Michael.

LDP: Of everything you've ever written, what was your favorite?

JM: That's kind of like asking a father to choose his favorite child. Every story is a product of what's going on in your life when you write it, and as such, they're all important, and they're all special. That's not a cop out. It's the truth. But when people ask for a book that will introduce me to them as a writer, I always point them to Apocalypse of the Dead. I pulled out a lot of tricks for that one, and I think it shows my range as well as anything else I've written.

LDP: Do you have any tips on editing that you would like to share?

JM: Sure. Paraphrasing Hemingway, every writer needs an internal bullshit detector, and they need to listen to it every time they write. But a more practical tip would be to look at the multitasking potential of every scene you write.

For example, every scene and structural element should do at least two things at once. Dialogue should advance both plot and character. The setting should create mood and sense of place. There are countless other examples, but they all amount to the same thing. If you're not pushing your writing on multiple fronts, really thinking about what you're doing when you write and why storytelling works the way it does, all you're doing is creating a completely forgettable reading experience. My best advice? Slow down. Focus on the craft. Publish something that's truly badass, instead of merely publishing.

LDP: What are your pet peeves or "issues" with grammar?

JM: Nothing particular. But this gets back to what I was saying earlier about turning in a professional work product. I don't care if the rough draft is full of bad grammar, as long as the final version you show me is clean. There's just no excuse for freshman mistakes in grammar. Remember, you want to be treated like a pro, act like a pro.

LDP: Laptop or desktop computer? Which do you prefer?

JM: Doesn't matter a bit to me. I write all my rough drafts by hand. Everything after that is just typing, and I can do that on a laptop, desktop, IBM Selectric III, whatever.

LDP: Do you listen to music while you write? If so, what?

JM: No, I have to have everything quiet when I write. I find it's too easy to let my mind wander when there's music playing. I find the silence helps me focus.

LDP: What time of day do you write?

JM: Because I work a full time job and have a young family that demands a lot of my free time, I have to sacrifice a good amount of sleep. I get up at 4:30 and write until around 6, then again after the kids go to bed, which is usually around 8:30 at night. Because my time is divided like that, I find it works best to have a detailed outline in place before I start writing. That enables me to pick up where I left off pretty easily.

LDP: Are you an "in the zone" writer, or one that can sit down and write whenever you want?

JM: That's the nice thing about being organized and writing from an outline. When I get time to write, I have to be prepared to take advantage of it. Because I outline, and approach writing in a fairly organized way, I'm almost always ready to roll when I sit down at my desk.

LDP: Is there anything I didn't ask about that you would like to share with us? Any plugs?

JM: Well, my big releases coming up include my abandoned building anthology, The Forsaken, my horror novel, The Red Empire, and the third book in the Dead World series, Flesh Eaters. All of those titles are due out in April. On other fronts, I'm going to be moderating the zombie panel at the 2011 World Horror Convention in Austin this April. Also, I'm the Chairperson for the Horror Writers Association's Single Author Collection Category of the Bram Stoker Awards.

LDP: Thank you for sharing! Best of luck with your books!

JM: Thank you! I had a blast.

18 Ways
by Jim Bronyaur

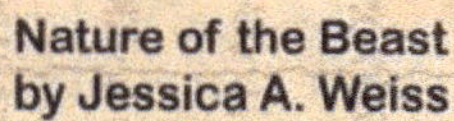

A hand from the ground.
The cool breeze on the back of your neck.
A light tingle on your neck.
 Is that glass?
 A spider?
 A fang…
Where did that breeze come from?
The broken, shadowed reflection when one light burns out.
The flicker of a candle that wasn't lit a minute ago.
The echo of your footsteps calling back on long, dead night.
The eyes in the bushes.
Brakes squeaking – there's no vehicle in sight.
The distant thunder.
The flash of lightning showing life in the dark.
The crack of thunder close enough to rattle your heart.
The branch tickling the window.
The wind pushing the glass.
Your mind.

Undead in Haiku
by Matt Nord

Death comes to us all.
A Rider on a white horse,
With his sword in hand.

My lips rot away.
My smile is eternal,
Yet I feel no joy.

Dead sit lamenting,
Of their lost humanity.
Why has God left them?

Frozen dead gaze out,
Longing to thaw, wanting flesh.
Springtime is coming.

Maggots crawling 'round,
Try to dig out of the ground,
Resurrection Day.

The living dead rise.
Yearning, hungry for fresh flesh.
Hear their gnashing teeth.

Walk across the street,
Check on my elderly mom,
She's a zombie now.

Cracked lips break open,
Revealing broken, brown teeth.
Let me taste your skin…

Waking up screamin',
Undead are a' chasin' me.
Can't sleep! Help me, Dad!

Survival is the key.
We cannot submit to them.
We must persevere.

Nature of the Beast
by Jessica A. Weiss

Every effort of his has been belittled.
People tell him he should be ashamed.
Growing up taught him to be cautious,
He'd always known he was a born killer.
There was no chance of his talents being wasted,
Enjoyment found with each new assault.
Most would consider his artwork revolting,
But nothing could disillusion him now,
He knew many more had been slated…

"Simple murder wouldn't do.
You're done and over far too soon.
Slicing, dicing, can be nice,
But torture is the thing I like.
Eviscerated and hung to dry,
Russian roulette says who's next,
You'll all pay till the day I die.

"Its a specialized skill, my art.
Full of trivial do's and don'ts.
No one who sees can ever return.
I've had to intercept some complaints.
I take great pride in what I do.
There is no need to be envious,
Only a devil, such as I, could do this.

"The name of the game is murder and mayhem.
You grow unusually pale with my words,
Hard to imagine all this done by one man?
To me, bleeding freely is an art to the lost.
No forces of man matter in my life now.
There is no end of the evil deep rooted in me.

"Bad blood flows in these veins,

Only seen as something ugly.

Always hearing them scream, 'No!'

Desires to kill bloom until sated.

Evil such as I will never die,

I thrive on prying eyes revolting!"

The party ended with a deadly crash!
Injuries sustained leaving a bloodied gash.
Full moon causing a nocturnal prowl,
Chomping on flesh with a satisfied growl.
Inherent habits have taken control.

Thirteen Questions with Blitzkid's Argyle Goolsby
Interviewed by Kevin Millikin

For many people the horror punk genre rests solely on the shoulders of such bands as the Misfits or the Cramps, but for the last 14 years, Blitzkid has paved the way for countless others, releasing 6 albums and numerous EP's and singles. They've done it all, from playing small clubs to headlining festivals and appearing in Gris Grimly's 2006 short film "Cannibal Flesh Riot" while also receiving favorable reviews in the likes of Rue Morgue and Horror Hound, which is why it's an honor to have the opportunity to interview Blitzkid bassist and vocalist Argyle Goolsby.

KM: 2011 marks the release of Blitzkid's latest record "Apparitional," the first since 2006's "Five Cellars Below." While "Five Cellars Bellow" was an incredible record in its own respect, what can we expect from the latest release?

AG: "Apparitional" definitely picks up where Five Cellars Below left off in that the exploratory direction we've always had is still in place. One thing different about this new record compared to Cellars, is that while Cellars had a very mid-paced tempo overall, the new record harkens back to more punk beats and elements that we first cut our teeth on.

KM: For the last couple of years, videos of new songs have begun to surface on You Tube. For songs like "She Won't Stop Bleeding" and "Jane Doe #9," is this typical of Blitzkid to try out new songs years before they're recorded to see if this one or that one becomes another "classic fan favorite"?

AG: We never try our songs solely to see what kind of reaction they get. At least not in the sense that we decide to play them—or not—based on crowd reaction. If we're recording a song, or we wrote a song we like to play amongst ourselves, then we're going to play it regardless of if anyone else likes it or not. It's important for us to believe in what we're doing and like what we're playing more than only doing something in the hopes someone else will like it. Naturally, we prefer to play the songs that get the best reaction, but lucky for us our audience seems to be in tune with what we like ourselves so that usually ends up making a cool set list.

KM: Nathan Bane from the band "The Epidemic" recently joined Blitzkid. From the beginning, both Blitzkid and The Epidemic were closely associated with one another. Will his involvement extend beyond Nathan being just the second guitarist?

AG: Absolutely. We've known Nathan since he was 14. He's from Cincinnati, a place we used to play fairly regularly before our bigger tour routings formed. He used to come to our shows and I would sneak him in because a lot of the times he was too young to be admitted. Nathan is one of the brightest, sincerest people I've ever met, not only in how he deals with people, but in how he approaches music. He loves music to the same degree that all of us in Blitzkid do. When it came time to look for a second guitarist, like we'd intended to do for a while, Nathan was our first choice. Luckily, he was down for the idea and is currently a huge force of progress in the band.

BLITZKID

KM: "Apparitional" is set to be released via "People like You" instead of "Fiend Force" Records. What brought on the switch, and what's it been like working with the new label?

AG: Fiend Force was and is a great label! They're some of the coolest dudes we know. They genuinely care about this scene and want to see their bands succeed. Over the years, Blitzkid has just kept getting more momentum and essentially grew into a band with needs beyond what Fiend Force could provide. I said they're all about their bands succeeding and their support and understanding of us taking the deal with PLY is proof of that. We'll always be thankful to Thorsten and Paddy at Fiend Force and we'll always remain friends. Thorsten is in a great band himself (The Other) and he knows what it's like for a band to need to grow. PLY is a very cool label! They're working as a subsidiary for Century Media Records and those guys are equally as cool! They're very approachable people and they get it. PLY has a passion for music that's backed up by great resources. We're really happy with the switch to their label. They're going to be instrumental in a lot of the progress you're going to see in Blitzkid this year.

KM: When can we expect to see the reissue of Blitzkid's back catalogue?

AG: Every record we have ever recorded, released and unreleased for that matter, has been picked up by PLY and will be released throughout the coming years.

KM: Can you give us any clue as to when we'll be seeing the release of "Anatomy of Reanimation Volume 2," and what we can expect to see on it?

AG: Don't hold your breath on that one. While it was a great experience for us to re-record those songs, retrospectively speaking, I don't think it's something we'd want to do again. There are a few reasons for this. First, it seems like no one understood why we were doing it to begin with, even though we stated clearly that we weren't re-recording the songs because we felt like there was something wrong with the old ones. People were put off that we were re-recording what they felt were classics didn't need to be touched. Though serious in our approach, it was purely for fun! We never had the chance to record those songs in a way—PRODUCTION WISE—that we were ever really happy with. We were really rushed through all of the albums that people to this day say are their favorites. That's the irony. At the time we decided to record ANATOMY, we were in a place as a band where we were ready to record a new album of new songs, but weren't in a place in the industry where we felt we were going to get proper exposure. So we put the brakes on for a bit to retool existing contacts and work on new ones that could make the most out of what I feel is our best album. We found those contacts. We recorded "Apparitional." And now we're in the right place to go forward. This is why we've taken the long course.

KM: Being an American punk band, has it been hard touring and supporting yourself stateside while most of your music is released and is also primarily available to a European audience?

AG: Yes. But this is one of the reasons we put the brakes on the band's progress when we did. We realized we were becoming a band dominant in the European market—for which we are and always will be supportive of being—but we weren't making the same progress in our own country. This was because of the aforementioned missing pieces on an industry level in this band. Fans are going to see a completely new Blitzkid with the release of "Apparitional," in the sense our songs will be available to the US market for the first time in the same way we've been made available to the European one. We're really excited about that.

KM: Can we expect a proper US tour in support of this release?

AG: 100% yes. And like nothing we've done before. We have the right label stateside, the right press contacts, awesome management (Riot Rock Management) and a brand new van!

KM: A few years back, I truly fell in love with horror punk while living in Austria/Germany where horror punk seems to reign supreme. Why do you feel these genre/lyrical concepts have caught on there while remaining such a small scene here in the states?

AG: I don't want to speak as if I know the preexisting social conditions of Europe, being that I'm not a person who has come from this culture outside of being a few generations removed, but if you really want to look at it closely, America has always had it served up to them. We're always constantly on the cutting edge with pop culture as it seems to be the main cultural influence in general. Europeans haven't had it that way. Their culture is much different and much more clandestine in many ways. Music and genres can become sensory overload here and a drop in the bucket in a world of art-turned-marketing. Europeans get the artistic value of it, minus the marketing-as-art seems to be much more of an integral part of their culture in general. There's something genuinely stark about the imagery and context around horror rock. I think it presents a visually artistic value on top of its musical value that may appeal to that longstanding appreciation for art.

KM: You've written some of the best horror punk songs in the last decade as well as been a part of such bands as Gorgeous Frankenstein (with ex-Misfits guitars Doyle Von Wolfenstein and drummer Dr. Chud) and 1476. What is it that draws you to the horror imagery even after all these years?

AG: First off, thank you. It's been a blessing to have what I've felt and expressed to be considered something of such value. I don't know really, I just get it. It's like that old Cinnamon Toast Crunch commercial where the parents ask the kids why they like that kind of cereal, and the kids would say, "We just do." Yeah, I'm going over a lot of people's heads with that one (except the old folks). As a kid, I loved the concept of man being interposed with bestial, natural, and purer elements than himself. How that—combined with forces of nature—either being a juxtaposed animal hybrid or assimilating qualities of nature like an unbiased-ness to life, made him a monster when in fact he was more of a creature of nature as a result. Factor in that I fit in NOWHERE in the social hierarchies of my youth, and a direct connection was made.

KM: Like many other horror punk bands, Blitzkid has released songs inspired by classic horror films (Nosferatu, Hellraiser & The Hills Have Eyes). What are some other films that inspired you that haven't made their way into a Blitzkid song?

AG: Strangler in the Swamp, Metropolis, Cocteau's Beauty and the Beast, Mechanical Man, Day of the Triffids. The list goes on.

KM: What are some of the books that have inspired you?

AG: Packman's Model, The Colour of Space, Beyond the Wall of Sleep, The Picture in the House, and just about anything else by HP Lovecraft. The Gold Bug, The Raven, Murders in Rue Morgue Magazine, and much more by Poe. Poems by Baudelaire, Ewers, and old vampire stories like Varney the Vampire, and Carmella. I also love M.R. James. Stories like Whisper and I'll Come To You My Lad, one of the scariest stories ever written and interestingly enough where the concept of ghosts looking like sheets came from. I also love stories like The Willows and The Windigo by Algernon Blackwood. I love Sheridan Le Fanu. Wikie Collins, "What was it" by Fitz-James O'Brien is amazing. I also love Ralph Kram. Especially "In Kropfsburg Keep." I love all the old Victorian ghost writers. Lord of the Flies by William Golding, and one of my favorite books from an early age is Siddhartha by Herman Hesse.

KM: In closing, what can we expect to see from both you and Blitzkid in the New Year?

AG: Initially, a lot of changes in the sense that we've undergone some lineup changes, but the heart of Blitzkid lies in an awareness of its existence and our eye is "still" on that existence. When the existence if no longer full of life or vitality, then it's time to pack it up. But we're not there and no matter who comes and goes, the band is bigger than any one member, and as long as those that remain still live in the words and the stages we inhabit, then Blitzkid is in no danger of demise. We hope our fans enjoy our new album, "Apparitional." Check them out online at:

www.blitzkid.com and   www.myspace.com/blitzkid

Night Terror
by Darren Gallagher

Adam and Shamiya went out for dinner with a few of their friends. They had a good night and then came home. Shamiya went straight to bed; she was exhausted and was asleep as soon as her head hit the pillow. Adam sat on the bed next to her; he wasn't tired so he read his book for over an hour and then decided to try and sleep. He lay down and wrapped his arms around Shamiya, it felt good lying against her, but he still felt no urge to close his eyes. He became restless and turned away from her; he lay on his side facing the window. Suddenly there was a loud bang from inside the house, but only he and Shamiya were there, so he thought it must have come from outside and he was mistaken. But he started to wonder if someone was in the house; he looked toward the door, which was only a few feet from the bottom of the bed. In his mind, he saw the door opening, revealing to him something horrible standing, waiting for them. He was scaring himself so much that he put his head down and pulled the blanket over himself. As soon as he started to relax, he heard the door handle turning. Fear shot through his body like lighting. He pulled the blanket off his head and looked at the door. The handle was moving slowly downwards, and he wasn't imagining it this time. Ever so slowly, the handle descended and he lay there and watched it; he was too frightened to move. When the handle reached the bottom, the door slowly crept inwards. It was more than halfway open and he could see out into the hallway–nothing was there, but still the door continued to move longingly toward him. He began to panic and his breathing grew deep and heavy. What's opening the door? he thought. What's out there? What is it? Shamiya stirred and startled him; he jumped away from her. When he did, he could see out past the door into the hallway, there was definitely nothing there, but he felt like there was. He launched out of the bed, grabbed the door and slammed it shut so hard that it woke Shamiya. She opened her eyes and saw Adam standing with his back to the door, breathing heavily and looking terrified. "Adam, what's wrong?" she asked, but he didn't responded; he never even looked at her. "Adam?" she asked again; still nothing. She was beginning to get a little worried because she'd never seen him like this before. "Adam, what is it? What's wrong?" Silence... "There's something out there," he said finally, only his words acknowledging her. "What do you mean? What's out there, Adam?" "I don't know…but it's not human." He turned slowly toward her. His eyes were bulging out of his head; they were so huge that they scared her. She sat up in bed, pulling the quilt tight to her chin, pressing herself back against the headboard.She watched him. The expression on his face was so terrifying that she didn't want to; he looked like he was possessed. "Adam," she said, "what is it? Tell me what it is!" "I don't know," he said, the fear vibrated his voice. Suddenly there was a loud thump on the bedroom door. Shamiya shrieked. Adam jumped away from the door, then immediately went back to holding it shut, even though it was caught on the latch. Another thump–this one louder than the last. Shamiya screamed again but Adam never budged. Again a thump, and another; they were getting louder and faster each time. Shamiya sat on the bed terrified and screamed with every thump. Adam stood against the door petrified. "Adam!" she cried out. "Adam, what is it? Who's out there?" Suddenly a high-pitched wail invaded their ears and deafened them. The sound had come from the hallway, beyond the door. They put their hands over their ears, but it was no good; it was far too loud to block out. The wailing stopped but they could hear nothing except for the ringing in their heads. Adam felt something wet on his hands so he took them away from his ears and looked at them. Blood–his ears were bleeding. He looked over at Shamiya and she was peering down at her hands as well. He called out to her but she couldn't hear him. Suddenly the door busted open and threw Adam across the room, his head bounced off the wall and his vision went dark. Shamiya sat on the bed horrified as the room flooded with light, she put her hands in front of her face to protect her eyes. The light began to fade and she could see something appearing in the doorway. The evilest old woman she'd ever seen was floating there. Her hair was white and hung over her face–Shamiya couldn't see through it–her clothes were as white as her hair. Again the old woman wailed and it pierced her ears. Shamiya cried out in extreme pain and looked across the room at Adam–he was lying in the fetal position with his hands clasped over his ears. "Adam!" she called out, but she couldn't even hear her own voice over the old woman's wail. Suddenly the wailing stopped and the old woman began floating toward the bed. Shamiya tried to move away but only got closer to the headboard. Adam's vision had now returned and he lay on the ground staring up horrified as the old woman floated above the bed and hovered over Shamiya. He could no longer see her–she was behind the old woman. He tried to get up, but the excruciating pain in his head made him collapse back onto the floor. The old woman wailed again, louder this time, and the light that was radiating from her grew brighter. The wailing continued to grow in volume and intensity, and Adam struggled to look up at Shamiya–he could just make out the blankets moving on the bed and he knew she was squirming like he was. Suddenly the room went dark and the old woman was gone. What was that? he thought. Where did she go? Adam fought through the pain and pulled himself up onto the bed. Shamiya's eyes were wide and full of pain. He got closer and looked deep into her eyes, but she continued to stare straight past him for a moment before looking down at her stomach. He followed her gaze and saw the dark patch that was spreading out from between her legs. "What the hell?" he asked, horrified, but didn't hear anything. He feared the worst and pulled her up out of bed. They made their way out of the bedroom and into the hallway slowly–she wasn't doing too good and he was really worried about her. He picked up his keys, and half carrying Shamiya, they left the house; he put her in the car and drove to the hospital. At the hospital they shared what had happened, but it seemed like no one believed them–they just looked at them as if they were crazy. The doctor's informed them Shamiya'd had a miscarriage. The news devastated them even though they hadn't known she was expecting. When they told their friends about what happened, some of them said it was a Banshee. But it couldn't have been a Banshee…, could it? And if it was, why had she come after their unborn child?

Children need love, especially when they do not deserve it. --Harold Hulbert

Lewis Kalashnikov lived a dark life of infamy, lust, and the profane. The last year of his life, he reformed for the sake of his daughter and eventually died peacefully in his sleep. The first two anniversaries of his death were punctuated with an appearance of his corpse and an unexplained murder. Two days before the third anniversary, his only daughter found the one private detective in Seattle rumored to handle such matters. "Mr. Heller, I've been given to understand that you handle such matters and are quite the expert. Please help me." "Mrs. Kalashnikov, I'm rather involved in the aftermath of my last case," Heller explained. "I still have an inquiry to suffer through." Mrs. Kalashnikov sniffed softly and dried her eyes with a tissue. "Yes, I heard. You shot that horrible serial killer that mutilated those women. The city should be giving you a medal," she replied. "The papers don't seem to think so," Heller complained. "The papers don't understand that there are dark things in the world," Mrs. Kalashnikov said, with an unusual certainty that gave the detective pause. She locked her gaze into the detective's eyes. "I need your help, Mr. Heller." Heller was used to women clients flirting with him. It wasn't because of his ape-like face; it was because the clients were usually desperate. Before he married Joan, it was amusing and helped pass the time. Now, it was just irritating and embarrassing. "Look, Mrs. Kalashnikov, I'm serious about this inquiry. I might be out of business for good," Heller said. "The police are miffed that I got rid of their problem and the press found out. The press are milking the scandal for all its worth." Mrs. Kalashnikov nodded, stoically. Her face was perfect, like a Gibson china doll. She was in her late twenties, an excellent blend of adult and child features. She dressed in a crimson business dress with a matching hat and veil. Several times during the meeting, she crossed her legs to show off her shapely calves. She slipped her perfectly manicured fingers into her snap purse and produced a business card. "I trust that the moment this matter with the police is cleared, you will contact me," she said, knowingly. "Also, I might be able to put in a good word for you." The detective stood from behind his desk. Heller men were always tall, but Jake Heller had exceeded the usual family genetics by almost a foot; a giant among very tall men. Mrs. Kalashnikov nodded, not intimidated in the least, and stood. Despite her stiletto heels, she was only five foot five at the most. Grinning slyly, she slipped her card into his gloved hand and let her fingers linger longer than she needed. "Do you always wear gloves when you're indoors, Mr. Heller?" Heller resisted the urge to groan. "I had an accident during a case. I don't like people seeing my hands."

"I think I heard about that case of yours," she said, soothingly. "You saved someone, didn't you? Burned your hands? You're a bona fide hero, Mr. Heller. That's not something to be ashamed of…" Nervous, Heller quickly retreated backwards a step. Mrs. Kalashnikov smirked, satisfied that she could affect the large detective. "I can't promise it will be resolved in time, Mrs. Kalashnikov," he said. "But if the inquiry is over before the third anniversary, I promise I'll call you. Good luck." He cautiously moved around Mrs. Kalashnikov and opened his office door. "Joan," he said, calling to his wife. "Would you please see Mrs. Kalashnikov out?" Joan looked up from the accounts spreadsheet and grinned. She wore her brown hair short, her bangs kept from her eyes with a hair clip. She was lean, but athletic, contrasting with Mrs. Kalashnikov's petite, shapely frame. While Joan relied upon her naturally good skin and smile, Mrs. Kalashnikov used all of the modern feminine weapons of seduction such as make-up, lipstick, and hair styling. Joan knew that Mrs. Kalashnikov made her new husband nervous, which tickled and delighted her. While Joan escorted Mrs. Kalashnikov out of the office, Heller sat back down and started to softly beat his head on the desk. Amused, Joan couldn't contain her giggle. "Aw, come on, Jake. Did the scary little blond woman intimidate you?" "There was something weird about her," he protested. "What? I thought you private detectives always had hot women clients falling all over you," Joan said, smirking. "You could have stayed in the room," he replied. "She wanted to talk just to you. You have the reputation, not me," she said. "Besides, it was funny to listen to." "I might be out of business," he said, sadly. "I can't believe this. My grandfather started this agency. My great grandfather worked with the Pinkertons. You'd think all of those years would have earned my family some credit." Joan patted him on the back and kissed the top of his head. "Honey, you couldn't exactly tell the police the truth. No one would believe some writer sold his soul for a demon penis," she said softly. Heller lifted his head from the desk and started to crack a smile. "Oh God, it was hideous. And when he talked, it was like listening to it in stereo." "Where'd the other voice come from?" she asked. "You don't want to know," he said, wryly. She shivered. "Ick! I'm going to need to bleach my brain." "Yeah, and here I was hoping we could live a normal life," he said wistfully. "But I like helping people," she assured him. "Besides, our hours are flexible and I still have time to paint." "If they pull my license, we're screwed," he said. "I'll have to dig ditches or something." "I've lived without money before," she assured him. "I can do it again." He didn't reply, but just let his wife wrap her arms around him and give comfort. It wasn't easy admitting to her that the business was suffering. As more of his business shifted to matters of the occult, his regulars were starting to get nervous. The lawyers that used to direct business his way stopped answering his phone calls.

COUNT YOURSELF AS A SURVIVOR. . .
. . .AND YOU MAY NEVER ESCAPE

ZOMBIE ADVENTURE AT IT'S BEST!

"Maybe Miles will know what to do," he muttered hopefully. The front door opened and a faint hint of sulfur filled the air. An unassuming, balding man wearing thick glasses and a large red nose happily strode into the room. "Did I hear my name mentioned?" the minor demon asked. Annoyed, Joan picked up her can of disinfectant spray, shook it, and started spraying the room. "Can't you do something about that smell?" she complained. Miles sighed dramatically. "I'm afraid not, Mrs. Heller. You and your husband managed to defeat me, thereby changing my inner nature. While I might serve on the side of angels at present, I'm still a minor demon, with the usual limitations." Heller scratched his head. Joan was always a bit nervous around Miles, because once the minor demon had been after her soul. Turnabout was fair play. "What did you find out?" he asked. "You were correct. The demon that arranged for the deal with Mr. Wilson is quite unhappy and is targeting you and your business," Miles said. "And this won't be easy to recover from." "Who is it?" Joan asked. "Her name is Delilah, and she's my sister," Miles said. "She's my eldest sister to be exact. Spiteful, deviant, and feared by most of Hell." "I didn't know that demons had sisters. Is that going to be a problem?" Heller asked. "Well, you've already dishonored my family by defeating me. And let's be honest, your family has never had good relationships with the Dark One. In addition, you've taken away her latest toy, so I'd imagine she's the one behind the police department, the media, and the financial difficulties." "Can't you just undo what she did?" Joan asked. "Even if I lacked the morals that would prevent me from bribing and blackmailing the police, I can't match her power," Miles said. "Hell is the true metrocracy, only the most vile, cunning, and powerful fall to the bottom. One day, if she isn't stopped, Delilah will be an Archduke of Hell." "Okay, so obviously she has a lot of pull and power," Heller mused. "How do we stop her?" The phone ringing was the only answer. Joan answered it. "Heller Detective Agency, how can I help you?" Miles and Heller waited while Joan answered a series of questions with either a yes or a no. She glanced over to her husband confused, but pleased. "No, sir. No hard feelings at all," she finally said. "Good-bye." "Who was that?" Heller asked when she hung up the phone. "Detective Monroe," Joan said. "It seems that the fine city of Seattle decided the killing was justifiable and that your firearm license is now active again." "Interesting," Miles muttered, scratching his chin. "It's unlike Delilah to give up so easily." "Unless she could take advantage of it or a higher power stepped in," Heller said, glancing at the business card still in his hand. "You really think Mrs. Kalashnikov has the juice to make this happen?" Joan asked. "This wouldn't be someone related to Lewis Kalashnikov, would it?" Miles inquired. Heller nodded. "Apparently he died three years ago, and on the first two anniversaries of his death, he decided to pay a visit to old friends. Does that sound familiar to you?" "Indeed it does," Miles replied. "Lewis Kalashnikov was the only man in Seattle who was possibly hated more than you by the Children of the Dark One. It was rumored he bested the forces of Hell three times."

"So he was a good guy?" Joan asked. "No," Miles stated, while pouring himself a cup of coffee. "His soul was as black and nefarious as they come. He wanted power on his own terms. I never dealt with him personally, but I do know that he caused Delilah to be promoted in the infernal hierarchy." "Isn't that a good thing?" Joan asked. "Promotion implies closer to Heaven, Mrs. Heller. The scales are reversed in this case." "Other than power, the one thing that demons care about is status with other demons," Heller said. "So, should we just ignore the whole thing and hope it goes away?" Joan suggested, hopefully. "It never goes away," Miles said as he handed Heller and his wife each a cup of coffee. "And once you've shown weakness, they own you forever. I should know." Heller took a swig of his coffee. "Then obviously, we'll have to take the case and try to figure out what's going on." Mrs. Anstice Kalishnikov seemed unsurprised when Joan called her an hour later to inform her that the Heller Detective Agency would accept the case. She agreed to meet them at the tomb of her father. The Kalishnikov family had a rather large crypt on the outside of Lake View Cemetery. It was a cold autumn day in Seattle. The sun was barely visible under a cloud of mist and fog. Heller and Miles waited outside of the Kalashnikov Crypt. Heller lit a cigarette and paced across the path near the Lee family plots, which were the most famous plots in the cemetery. As a child, Heller loved Bruce Lee movies. Lee was already dead then, but he had evolved into a legend. That legend turned into tragedy when his son died decades later. "It's a real shame," Heller said, glancing at the Brandon Lee crypt stone. "I've heard a rumor that there was a family curse." "Indeed, I've heard much of the legend," Miles replied. "But if there was one in fact, I certainly never heard about it. And I'd expect someone would be bragging about it." "Is that possible?" Heller asked. "Curses that follow family lines?" "Are you asking about the Kalashnikov family or your own?" Miles inquired. Heller took another drag on his cigarette and coughed. "A bit of both, I suppose," he admitted. "I'm married now. I'm worried what I might pass on to children." "If there is a harmful curse on your family, I don't know it," Miles said. "But, there is a strange luck about you. You and yours tend to be a magnet for the strange." Heller put out his cigarette on a concrete stepping stone and then flicked it into the garbage. "My grandfather used to tell stories about seeing all sorts of wacky shit during World War II. I never believed him. Dad used to yell at him for scaring me," he said, wistfully. "But both of them had to deal with this crap, didn't they?" Miles removed his glasses and started cleaning them with his tie. "Indeed. Your father's activities are unknown to me, but your grandfather stopped a Nazi occultist from tearing a hole in the Great Barrier and reigning Hell upon the world," Miles revealed. "For ten generations, your family has had contact with the Children of the Dark One and not once did they become corrupt. That's relatively unheard of these days." "What about the Kalashnikov family? Are they cursed? Why would someone come back, like he has?" the detective asked. "Assuming that it is indeed his body, and that he is coming back under his own will, it could be any number of reasons," Miles explained.

"Perhaps, he had some nefarious plans that were incomplete upon his death. Revenge. Hatred. It certainly wouldn't be just to exist in that state." "Why is that? I'd imagine that any escape from Hell would be nice." "There is no escape from Hell," Miles stated grimly. "If it were possible to escape Hell, everyone would seek to do it. Hell is a state of the soul. For those tortured souls, seeing this world is just a reminder of all they have lost and shall never gain again. Akin to a starving man being forced to witness a banquet." The click-clack of high heeled shoes alerted them to the presence of Anstice Kalishnikov. Pleased, she grinned slyly. "Thank you for coming, gentlemen." "You seem awfully happy to see us," Heller said. "I'm putting my faith in you to resolve my father's issues so that he might be put to rest," Mrs. Kalishnikov said softly. "After three years, he deserves it." "Have you considered that your father might have arranged this?" Heller asked. The smile faded slowly. Her cheeks flushed. "Mr. Heller, my father gave up power, influence, and the ability to sustain his life because I begged him. He repented because of his love for me. I know that for most of his life, he was an evil man. But I assure you, he did not ask for this." "Fair enough," the detective replied. "We should check the crypt for evidence." She produced a key from her purse and gestured them to follow her. The Kalishnikov Crypt was a granite structure the size of a small house. There were two giant metal doors at the center of the structure. At the top of the doors was a compass intertwined with an eye surrounded by a great pyramid. She unlocked the crypt, stepped back, and Heller pushed open the giant metal doors. Stairs descended into darkness. "No one has opened the family crypt since we buried my father," she said, slightly nervous. Heller nodded and pulled a large black flashlight from his trench coat. He started down the stairs and Miles followed him. On both sides of the tunnel at the end of the stairs was a torch. Heller whipped out his lighter and lit both torches. The two flames dimly illuminated the underground basin. It was a large rectangular room with tombs inside of the walls. There were several display cases filled with watches, jewelry, and other keepsakes. "It used to be quite common to store family treasures like this," Miles explained. "It's downright unsettling," Heller complained. As he shined his light through the display case, he noticed an odd silver marble. The other items, like the pocket-watch, were covered with dust. The marble was spotless, and almost gleamed from the light. "Miles, what do you think of this? Someone must have put that here recently," the detective observed. "Oh my!" Miles said, gasping. "What is it?" Heller asked concerned. "That, Mr. Heller, is a Tempus. A small piece of eternity condensed into material form," Miles answered, awed. "Is it dangerous?" Heller inquired. "Very much so," Miles answered. "In the correct hands, the Tempus has the ability to change the world. I don't suppose you hear anything? Music, perhaps?" "No, should I?" Heller asked, worried. "I hoped that you would," Miles explained. "You and yours have always had a strange luck with the occult. I hoped it would mean that the Tempus had chosen you. Pity." "Tempus? Wait, you're talking about that story you told me about humans being touched by eternity?"

Heller retorted. "I thought you were trying to scare me." "Eternals are real. One of Kalashnikov's relatives must have been a Defiler. Couldn't have been a Sentinel, we chased them out of town twenty years ago," Miles explained. "So if a bad person with the right touch finds this thing, he could use it to hurt people, right?" Heller asked. "Defilers blaze potently, but briefly. Only a hundred years, but they leave their mark," Miles said, grimly. "Mr. Heller, you never want to meet a Defiler. Some go insane, killing and maiming as best they can. Others are methodical, mechanical. The demon hierarchy tries to give them a wide berth. Some manage to do so much evil that they are sucked through the Great Barrier and they merge with the nefarious in the universe and rule part of Hell." "Wow, that's certainly scarier than some poor schmuck selling his soul for a larger penis," Heller said, grinning. Heller handed Miles his torch and reached into his inner pocket. He produced a small set of lock picks and presented it to Miles as though he had pulled a quarter out of the air. "Well, maybe I'm not special enough for it to like," Heller replied, kneeling towards the lock. "But I can hide it for a while until it finds someone tolerable." "But Mr. Heller, that would be stealing," Miles chided. Heller slipped the pick into the lock and began to rotate it, looking for the proper sequence of the tumblers. He tried two combinations before realizing that his gloves were hindering his movements. "Don't look," he said. Miles nodded and politely looked away as Heller removed his leather gloves and stuffed them into his trench coat pockets. He tried a third time to pick the lock and was subjected to an electrical jolt. "Damn!" Worried, Miles focused upon Heller and caught a glimpse of his hands out of the corner of his eyes. His hands were horribly burned, leaving black, charred skin. Miles had seen many such tragedies in the past, many of which he had caused. Since mystically gaining a conscious, Miles found it difficult to witness the pain of others. "Are you okay, Mr. Heller? Your hands look horrible. Do they hurt?" Wryly, the detective slipped his gloves over his scarred hands. "Most of my sensitivity was lost. I don't feel much. I almost lost my hands completely, but a shaman was able to save them," he explained. "I have an ointment I use on them to keep them in good condition. Costs an arm and a leg, pun intended." "I wish I could have healed your hands as I healed Mrs. Heller's multiple sclerosis," Miles replied wistfully. Heller grinned, trying to put on a brave face. "Miles, I understand. You don't have the power to go against someone higher in the demon hierarchy. You've done so much for me and Joan. I appreciate it." "Yes, but what happens after the spell is over?" Miles asked, afraid. "It's like that movie we saw. The one where that slow man is made super intelligent. So intelligent and insightful that he knows the treatment won't last. He'll return to being slow again, but he'll remember forever what it's like to be smart." "Miles..." "Everything is different now. I understand why people like puppies. Living puppies that is. I know what friends are. How to enjoy a raining afternoon with a friend over coffee. Having friends instead of allies," Miles said. "It will all be over when my contract is over. I don't want to go back." "Miles, I don't know if anything can be done. You are what you are. But I think the fact that you're worried is maybe a good thing, you know.

Maybe you won't switch back. Maybe the magic will be gone, but you'll have learned good behavior," Heller replied. "But I promise, we'll look into it." Miles wipes his eyes, tearfully. "Thank you, Mr. Heller." "Thank me by breaking into this case," Heller replied. "Can you burn through the glass?" "That would be destruction of property," Miles said, shocked. "We can't just leave that thing in there. Someone evil might find it," Heller argued. "And then they could use it to hurt people." Miles started cleaning his glasses on his tie. "But this is a crypt. A holy place. Wouldn't it be wrong?" "Miles, look, I know you want to be a good guy, but this world isn't a perfect place," he explained. "Sometimes you do things you don't want to for the greater good." "Mr. Heller, I've used that exact line of reasons to corrupt people," Miles retorted. "The difference is that I'm telling you the truth. You can still smell lies, right?" "They smell like honey," Miles complained. "I keep meeting new people and then keep getting disappointed because the stench lingers." "Not every lie is a bad thing. Sometimes the truth can cause more pain than it's worth. You should know that from experience," Heller said. "Just like sometimes you need to bend the rules a little for a greater good." "Indeed, I do, Mr. Heller," Miles said, considering the argument. "Very well, please step back. And hold these torches. We'll see what I can do." Heller accepted the torches and took several steps away from the cabinet. "Do you think you can bust the magic on that?" Miles frowned at the implications. "Mr. Heller. I may be recently reformed, but I do have professional pride. Just because you happened to get lucky, you shouldn't underestimate my abilities. I've humbled thirty wizards in my time. Convinced priests to share the love that dare not speak its name. I've started wars, plagues, and the downfall of empires. I've whispered in the ears of Charlie Manson, cheered when the pilot released Little Boy on Hiroshima, and funded 'Istar.'" "Wow, you never told me about Istar," the detective grumbled. "There are some things you can never redeem yourself for." "I've met the real Ishtar," Miles admitted. "She's quite beautiful. Spurned my advances. It was the worst thing I could think to do at the time." "Maybe you should look her up," Heller suggested. "You aren't evil anymore." "She settled down in California and grows avocados now with some Aztec deity. Besides, I have a job to do," Miles replied, knowingly. "You'll need me more after the baby." An easy feeling trembled in his stomach. "Baby?" Despite himself, the minor demon smiled. "Just practicing lying. It is a skill like any other. One needs to practice." Miles summoned forth the hellfire. It flickered and danced upon his hands. The wild flames burned crimson and smelled of sulfur, but were cold. The flames of Hell lacked heat, but they burned with the intensity of ice, despair, and loneliness. Carefully, he placed his hand upon the display case, melting the glass. Shadows flickered around the crypt menacingly, giving an eerie glow to both their faces. Once the hole was large enough, Miles withdrew his hands and dissipated the hellfire. He took a step back and he bowed wryly. "At your service, Mr. Heller." "Aren't you going to grab the Tempus?" Miles began to clean his glasses once again with his tie. "I can't, Mr. Heller, demons and angels are not permitted to touch a Tempus," Miles explained. "I don't know why.

I only know that if we do, there are dire consequences." Heller rolled his eyes. Miles could be more superstitious than his grandma. Still, it was always good to be extra careful. He slipped his hand into the display case and plucked the Tempus into his hand. Pulling it out of the case, the detective examined the Tempus. It was difficult to believe that such a small thing could be so important and powerful. The metal seemed polished and perfect; he couldn't find a single flaw in the sphere. "We should keep it in the safe at home until we know more," Heller replied. "Good plan, Mr. Heller," Miles said, approvingly. "The unique surrounding may provide limited shielding from prying eyes." "Yeah, that was my thought, too," Heller admitted as he slipped the Tempus into his pocket. "Okay, let's do the job and get out of here." Amused, Miles handed Heller back his torch and stepped aside so he could lead the way. The detective followed the markers encased in the walls with ascending dates until he found the marker for Lewis Kalashnikov. Heller began to push against the marker, searching for loose stones or possible triggers. "If I were a magician trying to figure out a way out of my own grave, how do I arrange it? Magic?" "He would have no way of knowing how much magic he would be able to use once dead," Miles replied. "If there is magic involved, it would have to have been cast before he died and so would have to have a set activation trigger." "And, I'm guessing he can't talk too well, so it's not a voice trigger," Heller added. "He must have a trigger inside to get out. But I'd think he would be smart enough to also have one on the outside just in case," Miles replied knowingly. "Lewis Kalashnikov was a cunning man." "You did know him, didn't you?" Heller asked, angry. "You lied to us to protect us before, didn't you?" "To my great shame, yes," Miles confessed. "My sister and I turned him many years ago. He was just a student then, eager to learn. But he was cruel, power hungry, and a deviant. Some things are better not spoken." "Miles, I know you want to protect us, but you could really screw things up by not telling us everything," Heller said, earnestly. "If you're going to work for us, you need to have full disclosure. Otherwise, I'm going to have to fire your infernal ass." "Lewis Kalashnikov tricked the forces of Hell. He gained power without trading service. He was marked for death over a decade ago when he did a horrible favor for the Lord of Seattle," Miles explained. "And the Lord of Seattle is this MacDuff character right? The Defiler gangster?" Heller asked, trying to verify his information. "More than a mere gangster, Mr. Heller. Finneus MacDuff is more than a thousand years old and one of the most powerful Defilers to walk the Earth. He's a direct vassal of Mephistopheles, Prince of Hell," Miles revealed. "We can't think to attempt to lock horns with them." "I thought Eternals only lived a hundred years." "That is their natural lifespan. There are dark rituals where a Defiler may take the remaining time from another Eternal. The process consumes their soul." "What favor did Kalashnikov do?" Heller asked. Miles frowned. "Is it really necessary, Mr. Heller? Mrs. Kalashnikov is waiting for us." "It's necessary, but not right now," Heller replied. "But you did give me a good idea. Lewis likely wanted to make it so he or his family could get him out if he needed. Could he arrange a spell that would work for his daughter?"

"Perhaps, but do we want to expose her? If she is innocent of her father's crimes, we should avoid risking her," Miles argued. "Blood is often an important aspect of death rituals right? What if we got a small bit of her blood?" Heller asked. "Using her blood could mystically tie her to the ritual," Miles explained. "Again, not a good option if she's innocent." "You keep saying that," Heller retorted. "Do you have reason to think she's not innocent?" "I can not sense any malice in her soul, which means she's either a saint or maybe she can cloak herself," Miles revealed. "I didn't know it before because I was deceiving and it's hard to read the intentions of others when you aren't being truthful." "That certainly changes the landscape a bit," the detective grumbled. "Again, truthfulness is a job requirement. Is there an understanding between us?" "I apologize, Mr. Heller," Miles said earnestly. "I'm somewhat new to this and sharing information is anthem to my being, despite my new orientation. I will attempt to adjust." "Okay, then, let's assume there isn't a magical trigger for now," Heller said, thinking out loud. "If he had a mechanical trigger, let's assume it's hidden in the room. What kind of range of motion does a zombie have?" "Mostly the same as you and I, only not as spry," Miles answered. "So it would have to be something easy to do." "What if we're looking at it wrong? It's a puzzle right? What doesn't fit?" the detective asked. Miles began to read off the names inscribed on the walls. "Anna Kalashnikov, Demetrius Kalashnikov, Fawkes Kalashnikov…" "Fawkes isn't a Russian name, is it?" Heller asked. "Not that I know of, but a lot of your human names sound alike to me," Miles replied. "But that name does sound familiar." Intrigued, Heller examined that section of the wall. It was a newer addition and free of dust. He started feeling along the wall for hidden panels or switches. He fumbled around the inscribed letters until he found a pliable panel. "If this explodes on me, tell Joan that I said I love her and that I'm sorry for being a dumbass," he said as he pressed the switch. The wall panel of Lewis Kalashnikov slid open, releasing the scent of methane and decay into the crypt. Heller quickly covered his nose. Miles didn't seem to be bothered. Dried fluids and flecks of flesh stained the dead shroud, but the marble slab was empty. "He was here," Miles revealed. "Maybe two days ago at the most." Heller clicked the panel again closing the wall. "Okay, let's tell our bad news to the client." As they ascended the stairs from the Kalashnikov crypt, Heller was glad for the burst of fresh, misty air. Anstice Kalashnikov paced across the entrance, smoking a cigarette. "Did you find anything out?" she asked. Heller thought of the Tempus in his pocket. "Well, we verified that your father's body is missing. I figure that's enough to start looking into the matter," he said. "However, if we're going to accept this case, you have to agree to full disclosure of all of your father's documents. We need everything unfiltered to get to the bottom of this." She flicked her cigarette to the ground and smashed it with the toe of her Prada boot. "I'll have the majority of the papers delivered first thing tomorrow morning. The important legal briefs will arrive at your office within the hour. Will that do, Mr. Heller?" "Yes, thank you," he replied. "Just one more thing. When we report what we discover to you, it might not be pretty."

"Nothing about this matter is pretty, I assure you, Mr. Heller," Mrs. Kalashnikov stated. She tossed the key to the Crypt over to the detective. "Use this in case you need to come back and examine the evidence." "Thank you, Mrs. Kalashnikov." "Call me if you find out anything," she insisted. "Of course, Mrs. Kalashnikov," Heller said. "My associate and I want to take a look around the cemetery. Do you need someone to walk you to your car?" She winked as though highly amused at the concept that she wouldn't be safe. "My driver is waiting for me. I trust I can ensure my own safety," she said wryly. Heller and Miles were left speechless as she sauntered away. "There's something down right unsettling about that woman," Heller replied. "She reminds me of my sister," Miles revealed. "That doesn't help," Heller retorted. "Hey, you don't suppose she is your sister somehow?" "No, I was worried about that at first," Miles admitted. "Mrs. Kalashnikov is quite attractive, but she has a couple of flaws. Nothing major, just a few blemishes and a small scar on her chin. Delilah is too arrogant to allow her forms defections." "Sounds like a frightening woman," Heller said. "Sounds like the two of you have quite a bit of a rivalry going." "It's not in the nature of a demon to love. Hate is the closest thing we have," Miles replied, sadly. "Okay, so we know that the body is gone," Heller said, changing the subject. "He could have gotten out on his own. If he did, do you think he would leave a trail?" "Perhaps. However, it would be difficult to track through a graveyard. Dogs would be useless. However, with the proper components, we might try an alchemy blood ritual," Miles suggested. "How would that help us?" Heller inquired. "The primary principal of alchemy is that like attracts like. We have a sample of the fluid Mr. Kalashnikov was leaking in the crypt. We could use that to attempt to locate the rest of him," Miles answered. "However, some of the required ingredients are somewhat rare. I only know of one place in Seattle that would sell them." Heller's hopes faded. "Ye Olde Curiosity Shoppe, right?" "It's unfortunate that you offended Mr. Borri," Miles said. "He may still sell to you, but I suspect it would attract his attention." "Well, you have to admit, he did fit the profile of a serial killer," Heller protested. "And he didn't have an alibi." "True enough, Mr. Heller, but Remington has lived a thousand years and is used to being treated with respect," Miles said. "You insulted him in front of his customers. He'll seek revenge; though doubtless it will be indirect. Remington has survived by being subtle." Heller thought for a few moments, while scouting around the Kalashnikov family crypt. "What if we use a third party?" Miles considered it. "You're thinking of Loxi Collins, yes?" "She helped us with the serial killer," Heller argued. "Maybe she'd help us again." "She's also half VuTente demon. One of the most powerful breeds of demons that walk the planet," Miles explained. "VuTente are temptation demons. They deal in vices." "She owns a coffee shop," Heller protested. "That's hardly a crime in Seattle." "I'm merely advising caution, Mr. Heller. We don't know exactly what her other affairs are at the moment. She wasn't a big player, but her breed is often subtle." "If you have a better idea…" Miles didn't. Curious and lacking other leads, they drove to the U-District. It was late afternoon and the street rats were out in force. Dozens of pierced, scruffy-looking teenagers with a variety of hair colors unknown in nature, dressed in baggy clothing, were wandering the streets.

They were chatting, hanging around, and generally enjoying the summer day. Loxi's coffee shop, Apropos, was on the corner of University and 55th. The area was named after the University of Washington campus and the university's presence could be felt in the used music stores, the Husky t-shirt stands, five teriyaki chicken restaurants, a tattoo parlor, a comic book store, and a dozen coffee bars. There were several empty lots and closed-down businesses. The atmosphere of Apropos was lively. There was a stage in the front corner where someone was reading poetry from an open microphone. A few people watched the performer. In the other corner, near the entrance, there was a row of laptop computers that patrons were using. A little bit further back, there were a few steps leading to a slightly raised area that looked like it would be a great location for an in-depth conversation. Local art work was displayed on the exposed brick wall between the computers and the conversation area. Many of the café tables were filled with people. It didn't seem that unusual at first, but upon a second glance, Heller was surprised by how many of the customers had a supernatural vibe. Most of them were sitting side by side with regular people, drinking coffee, reading books or working on lap-tops. The other side of the building had windows which allowed for an easy view of the bustling Avenue and a mellow side street. Where the windows ended, there was the coffee bar and pastry display. Heller took a deep breath, the coffee smelling enticing. "Don't tell Joan I'm sneaking a pastry." "The doctor did warn you that you need to watch your intake, Mr. Heller," Miles stated. There was a woman behind the counter that was clearly the master of this domain. Her hair was a beautiful mixture of black and purple dreadlocks. She had a cute, chubby, heart-shaped face that seemed to beam innocence and enthusiasm. Seeing them, she smiled and wiped her hands on her brown apron. "Oh look! It's my favorite detective and his new sidekick." "It's a pleasure to see you once again, Ms. Collins," Miles said, bowing slightly. Loxi blushed as though surprised and giggled. She had a quality about her that made it difficult to guess her age. Heller would have estimated twenty-three at the oldest. However, Loxi could smile and suddenly all of the years and wisdom manifested itself. "Please excuse Miles, he's still getting used to social niceties," Heller said. "I've always had social niceties, Mr. Heller," Miles said stiffly. "I simply belonged to a different class with different rules." Loxi smirked, taking a long glance at both of them. Her eyes were normally green, but for a brief moment they flickered with purple specs of power and energy. "Chazz! Our guests will have a caramel macchiato and a soy sugar-free vanilla latte. Mr. Heller will also have a blueberry scone!" she yelled. A thin barista with dark wavy hair started making their drinks. "Right away, boss!" "Thank you," Heller said, a little uncomfortable. "Oh, come on, Jacob," Loxi chided. "All I do is look and see what you want. I don't hurt anything. And I provide the best coffee in town." Heller frowned a bit and nodded. "Sorry, didn't mean to be obvious. Just feels a little weird, you know?" "Well, at the least, both of you are polite," Loxi smiled. "Obviously, you're here with a purpose. How can I help you?"

"We're working on a case and we need some ingredients for a tracking ritual, Mrs. Collins. Mr. Heller is no longer welcome at Ye Olde Curiosity Shoppe, as you might be aware," Miles explained. Loxi chuckled. "You really did embarrass him. Don't worry, he'll do something minor to get back at you and then forget about the whole thing. Remington plays long term." "Will you help us?" Heller asked. "Sure, just get me a list of what you need. I'll have Chazz run over there," Loxi said. "Is he…unusual?" Heller asked. Loxi laughed. "No, he just fell into the truth. Kind of like you, except he doesn't have the family curse," she replied. "I'm sending Chazz because he's man-pretty and Remington falls for that sort of thing." Heller smacked his forehead. "No wonder Remington has been so offended at the accusation of him hunting down women," he muttered. "That was only part of it, but yeah, I imagine his revenge will be rather amusing once the storms over," Loxi said. "There's a rumor that a bunch of oracles have predicted the coming of a Sentinel to Seattle" Heller and Miles exchanged a knowing glance. "That's not possible," Miles argued. "No Sentinels can come to Seattle. The Prefontane Well has been dry for over a decade." "Wow, turn into a good guy and suddenly no one wants to gossip with you anymore," Loxi said, teasing. "Water started flowing in the well a few weeks ago. No one knows exactly why. Although I have an idea…" "This is good news! Good news! Though it might only be temporary," Miles replied. "Maybe, but things seem to be looking up," Loxi said, content. "I don't understand," Heller said. "A little over a decade ago, nine of the evilest bastards ever to walk the Earth came to an agreement to make Seattle a home for the Children of the Dark One," Loxi explained. "Seattle had all of the perfect ingredients needed to be the perfect dark city. Great weather. Underground tunnels. Large homeless populations. Close to the water. Everything was perfect except the people." Miles coughed, clearly uncomfortable. "Seattle has an innate spirit of hope. It's personified by the Blue Lady." Heller pulled on his gloves to ensure they fit tight against his fingers. "And the Blue Lady is one of them, right? Mystical personifications of belief?" "Yes, Mr. Heller. This one was extremely powerful and blocked many attempts by the Children of the Dark One to seize control of the spirit of the city," Miles said. "You were there, weren't you?" the detective asked. "I won't be mad at you. You were evil at the time." Miles cleaned his glasses with his tie. It was an excuse not to have to look at them. "MacDuff gathered us on the night that Kurt Cobain died. Thousands of humans mourned and grieved. Many of them were caught in despair. We knew that was the moment. We gathered at the Prefontane Fountain and we bound her spirit. The well died. Without the Blue Lady, we were able to sweep through the city, killing the remaining Sentinels and other elements that didn't want to play ball. To my knowledge, there hasn't been a Sentinel in Seattle since then." "But your magic changed," Heller observed. "You can't be part of anything evil. That might have broken the spell." "If that is the case, Mr. Heller, then the window is only temporary," Miles said, wistfully. "Maybe not. Who else was there? I've heard rumors, of course. But you know how it is. After a while, everyone takes credit for the really bad stuff," Loxi said. Mile's head began to turn bright red and sweat dripped from his forehead. "My sister, Delilah, was there.

She came representing the Demon Lord Asmodeus. She brought the Defilers Bryon and Murphy. I was with Finneus MacDuff's faction. My ex-boss, Mephistopheles, supported MacDuff's plans for the city. MacDuff brought with him the Defiler Christian Beron and the Alchemist Lewis Kalashnikov. The shaman Remington and the Defiler Bucky were the rogues not belonging to either faction." Heller nodded, suddenly understanding why Miles had been avoiding this case. Lewis Kalashnikov had been one of the nine that had damned Seattle into the darkness. In a real way, they killed the hope of an entire city. The last few years had been difficult for Heller. It seemed as though Seattle had become some sort of evil Mecca for monsters, killers, and fiends. Heller couldn't imagine having done the things that Miles had done over the years and still be able to care. In private, he would have a talk with Miles, but for now there was an opportunity. "I think we have a unique opportunity here. Loxi, you helped us before. Are you willing to help again?" Heller asked. Loxi curled one of her dreadlocks with a finger. She was a short woman, not quite five feet tall. She had an inviting, voluptuous body that might never be in a magazine, but had a special appeal. "I'm a lover, not a fighter," she said coyly. "But you care about what happens in this city," Heller replied. "I know you do. You didn't have to help us." "Maybe my business was being hurt by women being afraid to leave their house at night," Loxi suggested. "Or maybe, I was using you to get at a rival." "This city has changed, Loxi. We can all feel it. I thought it was just because I was married and in love," Heller said. He continued to pull his gloves tighter upon his hands. "I know people. Even people that aren't human. It's a gift. You want people to be happy. You want to be happy. You want to fall in love." "He's very good," Loxi said to Miles. "Think he's good enough?" "He tricked me. That's never been done before," Miles replied. "And he has a good, forgiving heart." "I'll help, as best I can," Loxi promised. "But you guys have to keep it on the downlow. I'm vulnerable right now." "Fair enough," Heller agreed. He placed a stack of twenties on the table. Spending the money would hurt in the short term, but he would charge it to the client and recoup the loss. "If Miles and I figure out a way to end this, we'll contact you. Until then, please send Chazz to buy the goods." "Sounds good to me,' she said. "With luck, Chazz will get the man-pretty discount. Be safe, you two!" The detective and the minor demon rode home in silence. Heller waited until he parked the van to speak. "Miles, look, I need you to tell me these things in the future. I get that you're ashamed, but I'm not going to judge you for what you did back then. But I am going to judge you for what you do now. Understand?" Miles forced himself to look into Heller's eyes. "Mr. Heller, I've never really had a friend, and while this may seem odd, I consider you my only friend." Heller laughed mirthfully. "Is that what this is all about?" "I've never had a real friend before. Not a someone that wouldn't stab in the back the first chance they got," Miles explained. "Real friends screw up all of the time," Heller said, smirking. "And the truth is that I don't have many friends either. I lost most of them after...after Kent and that boy. I lost my job on the force. Lost a lot people. You and Joan are really all I have."

"So you consider me a friend, too?" Miles asked hopefully. The van windows were starting to fog. Miles sometimes gave off excess heat when he was nervous. "Geez, Miles, calm down! It's like a freaking oven in here," Heller complained. Annoyed, he rolled down his window. "Yes, I consider you a friend, too." Miles smiled, wiping the sweat from his face. "Thank you, Mr. Heller. I appreciate that. But when I go back to being evil…" "Oh, I'll pop a cap in your ass, don't worry," Heller said jokingly. Miles and Heller left the van and entered the Heller Detective Agency in good spirits. Upon opening the door, they saw the piles of cardboard boxes scattered throughout the office. Joan Heller was searching through one of them, digging in the files within. Joan was short, maybe five feet three inches on a bad hair day. Her hair was short, brown, and had that special look that gives the impression she just crawled out of bed. From the dark circles under her green eyes, it was clear she hadn't been getting enough sleep lately. Upon seeing them, Joan let out a groan. "Going that well, honey?" Heller asked with a light touch. "I've been going through the records all day," Joan protested. "Wait until you find out everything we did," Heller teased. "The plot thickens, Mrs. Heller," Miles added. Joan smiled despite her obvious discomfort. She scratched her ears and then popped her neck. "Hey, I just waded through all this crap so I get to go first," she said. Heller chuckled and then nodded. "Sure, honey, go ahead." "It looks like Mr. Kalashnikov was involved in some sort of land deal with a local consortium," Joan revealed. "The plan was to build some sort of new age yuppie gated community. Around a year ago, he pulled out all of his stakes and sold his shares to the remainder of the cabal. Guess who they are?" "No idea," Heller answered, pleased. "Christian Beron, Finneus MacDuff, George Gordan, and last but not least, Gaius Remington," Joan said, smirking. "And guess who Mr. Kalashnikov visited last year?" Heller was too stunned to comment. "Who was it, Mrs. Heller?" Miles asked. "Christian Beron. Apparently the zombie broke into Devil May Care Software and trashed a bunch of computers," she said, pleased with herself. "The papers are saying it was just a guy in a costume, but I read between the lines." Heller lived for moments like this when all of the pieces of the puzzle fit together perfectly. "You said there was a land grab? Was it near the Prefontane Fountain?" he asked, excited. "How did you know? she asked, half surprised and half pouting. "Honey, we've been out hunting for clues. I feel like a caveman about to show his cavewoman a big freakin' wooly mammoth," Heller said. Joan started fiddling with her ear again. "Either I have a ringing in my ears or someone is playing music really low," she complained. "Did you bring me a music box?" Joan had a fondness for music boxes. She owned four of them. "I didn't bring…" Heller glanced over at Miles, remembering what he had in his pocket. Miles dropped his jaw with surprise. "Is it like bells, Mrs. Heller?" Joan thought a moment, listening. "Yes, and it's getting louder." Heller reached into his trench coat and pulled out the Tempus. Miles had said these things almost had a mind of their own and that they arranged to be found. Would it want Joan? Would that put her in danger? "It might be this," Heller said, holding the item. The music was clear now. It was beautiful, haunting. "What is it?" Joan asked, smiling.

Heller swallowed hard. Joan often helped with the research, but she had never stepped out onto a case before. How would this change his wife? He thought briefly about hiding it from her, but then put that thought away as selfish. She had to choose. "Miles said it was called a Tempus. And if you're hearing the music, then we have a lot to tell you." After Miles told Joan about Eternals, she stared at the small silver globe. "And so if I touch this thing, I become an Eternal?" Miles nodded. "I suspect that was why I was ordered to corrupt you. You've always had that potential." Joan put her hand on Heller's shoulder and leaned close. "Should I do it?" "Our lives are never going to be easy," he said softly. "That doesn't mean I should do it. What about kids?" Miles cleaned his glasses. "I don't actually know. The study of Eternals was never my vocation. Certainly, I've never heard of any Defilers having children."

"That doesn't mean it can't happen, though," Joan argued. Heller placed the Tempus on the desk and embraced his wife. "This could put you into more danger." "I won't do it if you say not to." Heller kissed her. "You were just saying this morning that you wanted to be more a part of this life." Miles sniffed sympathetically. "To be fair, Mrs. Heller, you'll always have the potential, which means you'll always be in danger. At the least, you would have increased power to defend yourself." Heller peered into his wife's eyes lovingly. "Do what you feel is right. We'll be okay." Joan accepted the Tempus. She expected to see fireworks or perhaps feel differently. "I don't feel any different." "Your aura has already changed, Mrs. Heller," Miles said. "I can already sense new reservoirs of power within you." Joan extended her arms experimentally. "So can I fly now?" Miles rolled his eyes as if to wonder how these two mortals managed to trick him. "I'm not intimately familiar with the abilities of an Eternal, but I do know that the Tempus affects each one differently according to their nature. Your guide will explain things better." "I get a guide?" "Indeed, Mrs. Heller, but the guide might not come if he or she senses my aura." "We don't have time to waste," Heller stated. "Mr. Kalashnikov is running around Seattle undead and might be feeling a bit ornery about it. Personally, I don't mind if he takes out some of the bad guys, but he might get some innocent people along the way." "Loxi said she would have Chazz bring us the ritual components," Miles said. "Okay, so what happens when we find him?" Joan asked. "Do we kill him? Can we banish him? Does that send him to Hell?" "Most zombies don't have souls. It's just flesh commanded to serve a purpose," Miles explained. "However, as this zombie is seeking revenge, it would seem that Mr. Kalashnikov's soul inhabits his body." "Is there a way to contain a zombie? Trap him somehow?" Joan asked. Miles nodded excitedly. "This wouldn't work against normal zombies, but if we encase Mr. Kalashnikov in a circle of salt, he'll be afraid to pass it or risk removing his soul from his body." Heller adjusted his leather gloves, ensuring they were snug against his fingers. "Maybe we can trap him long enough to figure out what's going on." "And then what?" Miles asked. Heller winked at the minor demon. "And then I do what I do best." As promised, Chazz delivered the components. His shirt was a bit disheveled and his hair was a mess.

Heller didn't want to imagine what Chazz had to do to get the materials from Remington, so he tipped Chazz an extra hundred. The agency couldn't afford it, but he wanted to be able to sleep when the case was over. Besides, Mrs. Kalashnikov had promised to pay all of the expenses. Miles polished a bowl crafted from silver and then nodded to Heller. The detective emptied the slime sample from the Kalashnikov family tomb and took a step back. Miles mixed borage, dill, and wormwood into the bowl and ground it together into a fine paste. Then, the minor demon pricked his finger and allowed a single drop of his blood to drop into the mixture. The needle pointed south. Miles grinned proudly. "I believe it worked." "Do we know how far we need to go?" Joan asked. Heller opened his desk drawer and pulled out his pistol. "It's a beacon ritual. The needle will point like a compass. We'll have to drive around to figure it out. You want to come along?" Joan squeezed the Tempus in the palm of her hand and squealed. "Me? You guys never let me go. Can I drive?" Miles swallowed nervously. "Mrs. Heller, it's somewhat important that we have a steady driver. And we don't know what effects the Tempus will have on you while changing you into an Eternal." Joan smirked. "Miles, surely you aren't that afraid of my driving?" "Mrs. Heller, I assure you that should I ever return to my former state, I will use my memories of our last shopping trip as a punishment to any that disobey me," Miles replied flatly. Joan stomped her foot in protest. "It wasn't that bad!" Heller checked the pistol to ensure it was loaded and slipped it into his coat. "Uh, guys, we have a zombie to catch that might be hurting people. Innocent people." Heller managed to herd them into the car without comment. Joan rode in the back, excited about her first ride-along. Heller drove while Miles reported changes in the direction of the needle. It was more difficult finding the zombie than they expected despite the tracking ritual. The needle pointed a general direction, but they had to navigate traffic, one-way streets, and the unique city grid of Seattle. Sometimes, Heller had to make several turns along the side streets to find the trail. The needle swiftly turned 180 degrees as they passed by First Avenue in Belltown. Miles managed to triangulate the location to an old brick building that housed offices, apartments, and a small pub. Joan was very confused. "Why would the zombie be here? Wouldn't someone see him?" Miles coughed discretely. "Mrs. Heller, that is the Butterworth building." Joan rubbed her hands together, excited. "That's one of Kalashnikov's properties!" Heller slammed the brakes and then swiftly backed into a parking spot. He gestured across the street to the strip mall. "He's set up in a position where he can strike at the cabal. Remington, Beron, and MacDuff are all within walking distance of this building," Heller said. "Shouldn't they know that a killer zombie is near by?" Joan asked. "Well, the rumor is that a lot of ghosts and spooks haunt this building." Miles nodded. "Indeed, the Butterworth Mortuary was in this building for many years and as such is very suitable for those interested in the necromantic arts." Joan grinned. "You mean like an undead alchemist trying to kill off all of his former buddies?" "Exactly, and if he kills Remington before the others, it could be a disaster," Heller said. "I thought we didn't like Remington." Miles carefully set the bowl on the floorboard.

"Mr. Remington keeps the others in check; certainly he's the most conservative of the council. I would shutter to think what they'd do without his influence." Heller checked his Glock once more and slipped it into his trench coat. "And hey, if nothing else, if we stop Kalashnikov, it might get the little bastard off my back." "How do we find him from here?" "The ritual won't work inside of the Butterworth building. Mr. Kalashnikov long ago cloaked the building when he purchased it and built one of his laboratories in the basement." "So if you know that Kalashnikov had a lab in the basement. Why didn't you just tell us?" Joan asked. Miles coughed. "Some zombies don't have the presence of mind that Mr. Kalashnikov seems to possess, and Mr. Kalashnikov had a dozen such places in the city. He liked to move around." "Yeah, right!" Joan replied sarcastically. "You just forgot!" "Don't be silly, Mrs. Heller, I'd never forget something like that!" "Hey! We have a job to do, remember?" Heller said. Miles and Joan looked at one another and then apologized. "Okay, Miles, take point," Heller said. They exited the car and circled the building, allowing Miles to get a feel for the area. There was a narrow alley behind the building. Joan gingerly stepped over the litter and broken bottles while Miles barely suppressed a smile. "What do you think, Miles?" she asked. Miles put his hand upon the painted brick wall of the Butterworth building. "There's a translocation circle near here, but I'm having trouble locating it. There's obviously a cloaking spell of some sort." Joan studied the wall and concentrated. There was an image hidden under the paint. "It's a stereogram. A hidden image. I can see a semi-circle right where you're pointing." "Are there any other images?" Now that she figured out it was there, Joan found it easy to spot the hidden lines. "There's a smaller circle with a weird sigil that kind of looks like a curved cross a few inches to the left of your hand." "Good job, honey! Is that one of your new Sentinel powers?" Heller asked. Joan rolled her eyes. "Jake! I did go to art school, remember?" Miles ignored their conversation and concentrated on finding the mystical power lines. With his hand in the correct location, it was simply a matter of activating the circle using his mystical energies. A whirl of energy sparked from the wall. "That should do it," Miles said as he pressed against that section of the wall and found that it had become soft and pliable. Within moments, his hand passed through the wall. "Shall we?" He disappeared through the translocation circle. Heller reached out for his wife's hand and gave her a reassuring squeeze, then they followed the minor demon. They stepped into a dark room lit by Bunsen burners. It was a fully stocked occult laboratory with a cauldron, pestle, and rows of shelves with bottles and jars of strange substances. On the far wall, there were rows of slabs where once the mortuary kept corpses. Miles stood before them, his hands arrayed in a defensive position. Lewis Kalashnikov, rotting and oozing, stood before them. He hissed and clawed at them, moaning loudly. Heller pulled out his Glock and leveled it at the zombie. "Mr. Kalashnikov, we've been hired by your daughter and just want to help you," he said. The zombie took a step towards them, swaying. It gibbered as though trying to communicate. It grabbed a bubbling beaker of green liquid and prepared to throw it. "He's going to attack!" Heller yelled. The zombie bellowed.

"Wait!" Joan cried. She listened to its strange noises. "I can understand him." "Mrs. Heller, you might possess true sight—the ability to understand. Can you understand me when I talk like this?" Miles repeated a series of foul sounds. "I'm not that bad of a driver!" Joan protested. "Excellent, you understood the language of Hell. We have a means of communicating with Mr. Kalashnikov." The zombie muttered. "He's in pain! He says his former friends betrayed him." Heller placed his hand upon his wife's shoulder. "Tell him his daughter hired us to help him." The zombie muttered again. "He can understand us. He doesn't want to go back. He needs to break the cabal." "That is highly illogical," Miles protested. "Killing the cabal won't release him from bondage to Hell." The zombie gibbered passionately. "Wait! That doesn't make any sense." "What is it?" Heller asked. "He said that he wants to escape from Heaven. It burns him. He wants to go to Hell." "He shouldn't be going to Heaven," Miles said with certainty. "He was an evil soul the likes of which is rarely seen." "And wouldn't Heaven be a good thing?" Heller asked. "Well, in theory, going there without being a good soul would be torture. I wouldn't know, of course," Miles said. Kalashnikov growled and gibbered. "He says that the light burned. To live on the hills and to have done what he's done is too much. He deserves the fire. He wants to pay for his sins," Joan translated. "So why kill the Cabal?" Heller asked. Kalashnikov grunted. "They changed his fate when they took an aspect of his power for their own purposes." Heller paced a bit, thinking. "No. They wouldn't have allowed Kalashnikov to run free if that were the case." The zombie waved his arms furiously and grumbled. "He says he can feel his power," Joan said. "There's a ritual that in theory will allow someone to take in a man's sin and their power," Miles explained. "The Sin-eater ritual involves a person who, through ritual means, would take on the sins of a dying person, thus absolving the dying of their sins while receiving the burden of the same. There are some Hoodan rituals that believe you can achieve a measure of the person's power via this method." Heller scratched his chin. Something was bothering him. "If any of the Cabal had absorbed Kalashnikov's power, there balance of power would have changed." "Who else would have access to such a ritual and access to Kalashnikov?" Miles asked. Heller grinned and nodded. Joan and Miles had seen that expression many times at the exact moment Heller solved a case. "I know who did this and how we can help Mr. Kalashnikov," Heller said. Anstice Kalishnikov arrived at the alley behind the Butterworth building as instructed. Heller and Miles were waiting. "Mr. Heller, I trust you have resolved the issue then? My father is at peace?" Heller nodded. "He will be soon, but we need your help first." He turned to Miles and said, "Miles, please open the door for the lady." Miles opened the portal and they escorted Mrs. Kalishnikov into the laboratory. Joan and the zombie were kneeling upon the floor, sketching a circle in chalk. Anstice's eyes swelled with tears. "Father! What have they done to you?" She rushed to her dead father's side and embraced him, ignoring the slime of his corroding skin. He muttered. The words were unclear, but the feeling behind them were not. "He asked why you performed the Sin-eater ritual," Joan translated.

Anstice blushed. "Father, I wanted you to go to Heaven. You gave up everything to repent and yet I worried it wouldn't be enough. And still, you suffer."

"Mrs. Kalishnikov, you seem to be under a misconception. Your father did go to Heaven and there he suffers," Miles said. Anstice glared at the minor demon. "What? That doesn't make any sense." "You can't just take away a man's sin and expect him to be ready for Heaven. You have to earn it. Imagine being there knowing the things you've done. Somehow, he managed to slip down once a year to try to set things right," Miles said. Anstice wept. "I gave up a piece of my soul for this! No! It can't be right." Heller knelt next to Anstice and the zombie. "And you still have time to make things right. To free your father. Surrender his power." Anstice gazed into the dried sockets of her father's corpse. "Can it be done?" "I believe it can," Miles said. "Although it won't be pleasant." "I'll do it. I'll do anything." While Miles talked Anstice and her father through the ritual, Joan and Heller left the laboratory for a breath of fresh air in the alley. "How did you know, Jacob?" Joan asked. "I realized that both the daughter and the father were making assumptions about why things were happening and that we bought into it. Once I figured out the proper motivations, everything fell into place." Joan kissed him. "Are you going to be okay with me being a Sentinel?" "I'm just sorry that you got hit with the Heller curse," he said. "You think all of this is a curse? You found me, saved me. I get to be one of the good guys now. We get to live a good life." "Yeah, but now you have to suffer through the trials. The weirdness won't ever stop," he sighed. Joan patted her husband's hand. "You'd better hope it never stops. I might get bored."

LDP: For starters, please give us some background information on how you came to be a writer.

ESB: I was pretty much born a fan of comic books and all things horror. After watching Romero's films as a lad and reading countless issues of titles like "The Legion of Superheroes" and "The Fantastic Four," I knew I wanted to try to give something back to the genres I loved. At the age of 26, I started submitting stories and my first two were accepted right off the bat. I've kept at it since then and I'd like to think I write stories that other fans like myself really want to read, that the mainstream doesn't always give us.

LDP: What are some of the titles of your books?

ESB: I've written around 35 books to date so I won't list them all. The most important one to me is "Bigfoot War" (Coscom Entertainment) which is my fanboy love song to all those low budget Bigfoot horror flicks we all grew up on. I swear it's my best book to date. Its upcoming sequel "Bigfoot War II: Dead in the Woods" is just crazy. It combines the Bigfoot mythos with the Z virus, and I won't even talk about how messed up the third book is. Some of my other books include "War of the Worlds Plus Blood, Guts, and Zombies" (Simon and Schuster), "Season of Rot", and my horror westerns "The Weaponer" (Coscom) and "How the West Went to Hell" (Pill Hill Press).

LDP: What are most of your books about?

ESB: I write mostly about zombies. I like to think I write "military horror" for lack of a better term. Though of late, I've branched out into horror westerns, superheroes, and of course Bigfoot horror.

LDP: What do you think people would like about your books and why?

ESB: The most common praise I get is that my work is very movie like and fun.

LDP: Have you had any other publications? If so, where?

ESB: I have had simply hundreds of short stories published over the years in everything from small press and Pro magazines to anthologies galore.

LDP: Where do your ideas come from? What inspires you as a writer?

ESB: Romero's films, the horror I grew up with, DC Comics, and just odd stuff.

I recently was dragged kicking and screaming into a hardware store by my wife to pick up something for the house and while I was there I saw this "thing" and it inspired the current novella I'm writing entitled "Into the Light."

LDP: As a reader, who's your favorite author?

ESB: David Drake is really high up there. It was his style I learned to write from. Also H.P. Lovecraft, Z. A. Recht, and Geoff Johns are among my favorites.

LDP: What's your favorite genre to read?

ESB: I read mostly comic books, and spend way too much money on them when I have to spend. If we're talking actual books, I read more zombie stuff than anything else.

LDP: What's your favorite genre to write?

ESB: Military horror.

LDP: What advice do you have for writers?

ESB: Never give up and don't lose your vision.

LDP: Of all the characters in your story, which is your favorite and why?

ESB: Right now I'm too emotionally invested in Colonel Drake from Bigfoot War II & III to name anyone else. Ask me again when I'm not working on a project and the answer might be different.

LDP: Have you ever co-written anything with another author? If so, was it a pleasant experience?

ESB: Yes. I co-write things often. I find it fun and inspiring. Stephen North and I wrote a SF zombie epic entitled "Barren Earth" back in 2009 and had a blast doing it. I also just teamed up with David Dunwoody for a superhero book called "Anti-Heroes."

LDP: Of everything you've ever written, what was your favorite?

ESB: "Bigfoot War." It's the most personal and fun thing I've produced to date. I also like to think it's original as it gives the Bigfoot Mythos an apocalyptic slant.

LDP: Do you have any tips on editing that you'd like to share?

ESB: I'm terrible at editing and proofing. My fate is usually in the hands of the publisher and their staff when it comes to that.

LDP: Laptop or desktop computer? Which do you prefer?

ESB: I hand write everything in a spiral notebook. Yes, I'm old school. Then I go back and type it all up, making changes as a second draft on my PC.

LDP: Do you listen to music while you write? If so, what?

ESB: Oh yeah. It helps me a lot. My current favorite music to listen to while working is Mumford and Sons' "Sigh No More" album.

LDP: Are they any plugs you want to let us know about?

ESB: Other than saying again that if you enjoy FUN horror, make sure you check out Bigfoot War and if you like zombie horror, please look up my older titles.

LDP: Thank you for sharing! Best of luck with your upcoming projects!

ESB: It was a lot of fun, you're welcome.

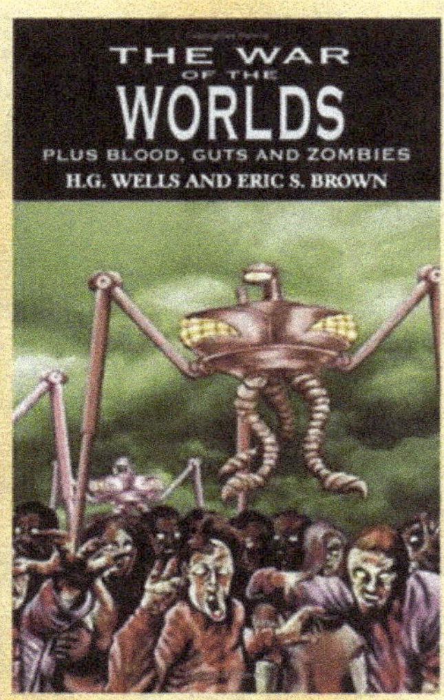

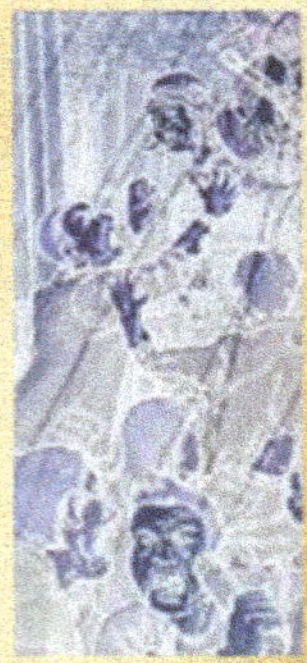

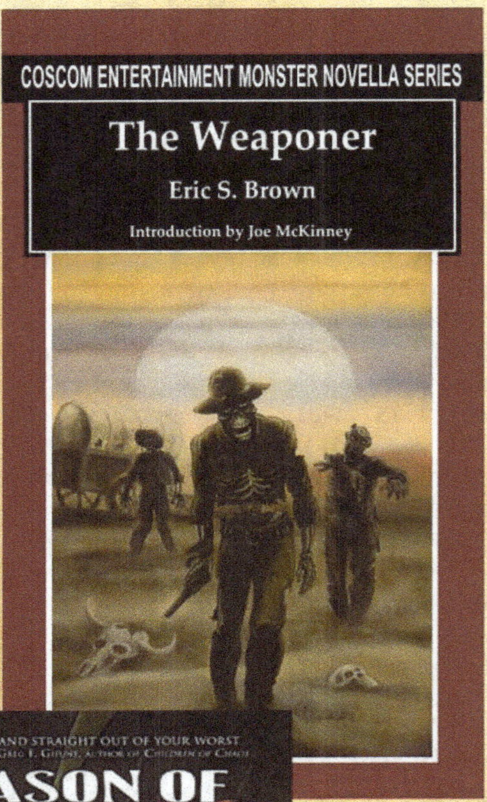

On Account of Bacon by Rebecca Besser

"Now tell me everything leading up to the events that got you arrested." I looked at the pompous attorney. I knew he wouldn't believe me if I told him. Silently I sat there, twisting my wrists back and forth inside the cold steel circles of my handcuffs, staring straight ahead. Sighing, the attorney looked up at me over the rims of his too-large glasses. "I can't help you if you don't tell me what happened," he said. I looked down at my lap, at my hands clasped together—knuckles white and jutting. I could feel my jaw muscles tightening, clamping my teeth together. I reared back, my chains clanging against the table and the legs of my chair, and looked this idiot-man-in-a-suit in the eye. "You won't believe me! Why should I tell you anything?" He blinked at me for a moment, withdrawing his hands from the small, metal table between us. "I'll believe you." But his eyes said he was lying. Biting my bottom lip, I thought for a moment. It might be worth telling this smug idiot the whole story, just to see his reaction. "Leslie?" "Okay," I sighed. "I'll tell you everything. You just have to promise to sit there and not say a damn word until I'm done." Sitting forward, I leaned my arms on the table. "Deal?" My attorney nodded. I could see he was confused by my abrupt mood change, but I didn't really care. Let him wonder. "Well, it all started when I was seventeen. My dad died, and my mom lost her job when the factory closed. She couldn't afford to take care of me, so I was sent to live with my mom's sister and her husband. My aunt and uncle lived on a farm. They raised chickens, cows, and pigs." The attorney raised his eyebrows and opened his mouth to speak. I held up my hands and shook my head. "You promised," I said. He nodded and shut his gaping hole. "Anyway," I continued. "I was sent to live at their farm. At first it wasn't too bad. Aunt Tisha was really nice and caring. Her husband was always busy with the animals. Their lives ran like clock work. Getting up, making breakfast, taking care of the animals, all the normal farming stuff. "When I first arrived, school was still in, so I was away from the house for the most part. I remember being eager for that summer to start. I had plans of getting a job at the local diner, waiting tables and having some spending money. I'd made lots of friends at school. Country people are actually as friendly as I'd heard they were." I smiled, thinking about the warm welcome I'd received at Riverside High. "It seems so childish now, how eager I was to have a summer of fun and freedom before my senior year of high school.

I was even thinking about what college I might want to go to. Some place fun, but that could also build me a good future through a decent education." Sighing, I lifted my hands to tuck my long, curly blonde hair behind my ear. The handcuffs were a pain. I had to remember to use both hands all the time instead of just one. I saw that one of my nails had a chip in it. "I was out of school for a week, working at my new job. Life was great. My mom even found a new job, so I was supposed to move back home in a couple of months. I was actually happy for the first time since before my dad died. Then it happened. I woke up early on a Saturday and I heard my uncle yelling at my aunt." I paused and took a deep breath. "He was yelling at her because she'd burnt the bacon. That's like sacrilege to Uncle Troy. If you burn the bacon, it's as bad as wrecking his truck or a tornado destroying the house. He was flipping out on her. I'd never heard him yell like that before. "I heard a smacking sound, my aunt scream, and then a thump. I raced down the stairs to see what was going on. I was scared, but I wanted to make sure my aunt was all right. I would have never gone down there if I'd known what was going to happen." I reached for the paper cup filled with water that had been placed on the table for me. I picked it up with a trembling hand and took a few slow sips. Setting it back down, I reminded myself to breathe. "It was horrible. Uncle Troy was standing over Aunt Tisha. She lay flat on her back on the floor in front of the stove. He raised his fist to strike her again, and she was crying and trying to wiggle away. "Aunt Tisha was a big woman, easily three hundred pounds. She couldn't move easily. He hit her hard, in the face. Then he hit her again as I ran through the kitchen, yelling for him to stop. With the second blow he'd knocked her out. "I grabbed his arm, still screaming. He pushed me away and kicked my aunt in the stomach, although she was already unconscious. I grabbed his arm again. This time he grabbed me by the hair and threw me into one of the hardwood kitchen chairs. It fell backward and my head hit the floor. The blow to the head stunned me, but I vaguely remember him correcting the chair and tying me to it. He tied my legs to the two front legs of the chair, looped the rope around my neck and then tied my wrists to the back legs. He had the rope run in a way that made it tighten around my neck if I moved my wrists or legs. I had to sit with my back arched, just to keep from strangling myself. He stepped into the laundry room and came back with one of his bandanas. He rolled it up and used it to gag me. "After he finished tying me, he went over and dragged Aunt Tisha off the floor and put her in a chair as well. He was extremely strong from doing farm work day after day. He moved her like she was nothing more than a limp rag doll. She started coming to while he was moving her, which seemed to please him.

"He used a roll of duct tape to imprison her in another of the kitchen chairs, growling and swearing at her. All I could get out of it was 'bacon' every few words. Mostly because he would scream the word at her. "The kitchen was filling with smoke from the bacon that was still on the stove, burning. Uncle Troy seemed to get more and more agitated as the smoke thickened. He started rooting through drawers until he found the silicone brush Aunt Tisha used when she needed to baste something. "The look in his eyes was psychotic. With a huge grin on his face, he dipped the brush into the bacon grease sizzling in the skillet. He turned toward Aunt Tisha and touched it to the tip of her nose. She screamed, shaking her head like a dog trying to get a bad taste out of its mouth. "Uncle Troy laughed. It was the most evil laugh I'd ever heard, causing goosebumps to break out on my arms and legs. "He dipped the brush in the bacon grease again, grabbed Aunt Tisha's hair, and held her head still. He brushed the hot bacon grease down across both her cheek bones, like he was putting blush on her backwards. "She was no longer screaming, she was shrieking like a crazy person. Her whole body was shaking with the effort to free herself from her bonds. I could smell her flesh burning. The scent mixed with the stench of burnt bacon. Every breath I pulled into my lungs made me gag. "I knew Uncle Troy wasn't worried about anyone hearing the shrieks and screams Aunt Tisha was bellowing. Living on a 300-acre farm, he knew no one would hear us, and no one would come to our rescue. "Aunt Tisha was begging him to stop, pleading between each massive sob that racked her body. It was terrible. He just kept dipping and painting, until all the skin of her face was fried. But the worst of it all was when he held her eye lids open and let hot bacon grease drip into her eyes. I looked away and wished I could disappear. The sounds she made were almost inhuman. I couldn't even imagine the pain she was suffering. I felt bad for her, but at the same time I was praying I wasn't next. "I thought the bacon grease in the eye was the worst thing he was going to do to her, but I was wrong. He picked up the entire skillet of hot bacon grease, opened her mouth, and held her head while he dumped it down her throat—telling her she could eat the crap she'd made. His body blocked my view of his actions, but I knew what he was doing, and I knew there was nothing I could do to stop him. I couldn't move without choking myself. I realized I was crying—my tank top was soaked with tears and I was trembling. "Aunt Tisha's body lurched violently. I heard strangling noises, saw one more violent attempt of her body to fight off the onslaught, and then she went still—too still. Uncle Troy placed the skillet back on the stove with a smile on his face and pleasure in his eyes."

I stopped talking and looked at the attorney. His expression was one of total disgust and blatant disbelief. I'd been there, I'd seen it happen and it was still hard for me to believe. I picked up my water and took another drink. My hands weren't trembling now. They were shaking, making it difficult for me to drink without spilling water on myself.

"He," the attorney said, clearing his throat before continuing, "he—your uncle—killed your aunt with bacon grease?" "Yes." "That's unbelievable," he said, shaking his head. "What happened after that?" Sighing, I closed my eyes and went back into the horror of my memory—the terror of that day. "I tried to be quiet, so I wouldn't draw his attention. I didn't want him to use the bacon grease on me next. I watched as he cut the tape holding Aunt Tisha in the chair, letting her slump to the floor with a thud. He kept mumbling something about 'poor piggy.' He dragged her out the back door and onto the covered, wooden porch. He left her lying there, with her feet still sticking through the doorway. "I heard his heavy booted footsteps as he walked around on the porch, as if he was searching for something he couldn't find. He swore loudly, and then I saw him strolling toward the barn; just like he was going out to milk the cows. Not hurried, but relaxed and enjoying the day. "I tugged my wrists and legs gently, to see if there was any possibility of me getting free. The rope grew tighter and tighter against my throat. I could barely breathe. I tilted my head back and sucked in as much air as possible. "I heard Uncle Troy's steps on the porch again, and watched out of the corner of my eye as he moved around Aunt Tisha's body. I heard cloth ripping. I saw her feet wiggle back and forth like she was being rolled over. Suddenly the feet disappeared. "I saw Uncle Troy through the window, throwing a rope over one of the thick beams that supported the porch roof. He tugged with all his weight. I could hear him grunting and swearing as he struggled with the rope. After a minute or two, I saw that he was hefting Aunt Tisha's naked body up to hang upside down. She was hung like the pigs after they were slaughtered. More tears fell from my eyes. My teeth were chattering from my fear and dread. Even though I didn't want to watch, for some reason, I had to know what was happening. It was almost like if I saw everything he did, I would somehow find an advantage that might save me. Even though every movement he made was more terrible than the last. "He came back into the kitchen, glanced at me and shook his head. 'You silly piglet, you're gonna hurt yourself,' he said. Coming over to where I was, he loosened the rope so I could breathe without my head tilted back, but still tight enough so my back had to stay arched. My whole body was aching from the effort of staying in that position. "Leaning down behind me, he whispered in my ear, 'I haven't forgotten about you, don't worry, you're gonna be next.' He kissed the side of my neck. I closed my eyes and tried not to scream. I didn't want to give him the satisfaction. "He turned and sorted through the knives in a wooden block on the counter, whistling under his breath. He must have found what he was looking for because he carried a couple of them outside with him. "Turning my head, I saw him walking around Aunt Tisha's body, thoughtfully. He nodded, and put one of the knives on the small table we used when we would sit and have afternoon drinks when we were relaxing on the porch. With the knife he still held, he started cutting into Aunt Tisha's stomach—just like I'd seen him do when he was gutting a pig or a cow.

He pulled out her guts, throwing them behind him into the brilliant green grass of the yard. They landed with a sickening plop. Scarlet blood flew through the air, dripped from Uncle Troy's arms, and streamed from Aunt Tisha's corpse. "After he'd removed her guts, he changed to the other knife. He slowly used it to cut off both her breasts, throwing them in the yard as well. He started cutting strips of skin and meat from Aunt Tisha's stomach. These went onto the table along with both knives. "He turned and walked off the porch again, this time around the side of the house. I heard the squeak of the outside faucet being turned on and soon I heard his boots on the porch again. He reappeared with the blue, rubber water hose. He began spraying Aunt Tisha as if she was nothing more than an animal carved up to provide food. After she was rinsed, he washed the strips of flesh he'd lain aside. "When he was done, he put the hose away and turned off the water. He gathered up the knives and the pieces, coming back into the kitchen. He dumped everything into the sink and washed the knives, putting them back into the block. He proceeded to wash his hands and get out a clean skillet. Placing it on the stove next to the old one, he turned on the gas burner. He laid the strips of flesh into the skillet one at a time, just like bacon. "I gagged at the smell that rose from his cooking. He turned at the sound and laughed. 'You don't like the smell, sweet piglet?' he asked sarcastically. 'It's just like a pig frying in a skillet. Just bacon. You like bacon.' I looked away and tried hard not to throw up on myself, knowing that if I did I would probably strangle to death. Laughing again, Uncle Troy turned back to the stove. "He turned on the radio and grabbed a fork from a drawer. He sang along to the country-western songs, flipping his 'bacon.' I closed my eyes and prayed. I prayed he wouldn't kill me or hurt me, and that it would all be over soon. "Uncle Troy spilled some grease from his 'wife-bacon' on the stove when he tried to drain it off; it splattered on the floor. He swore, stepped around it, and continued to cook. "When the wife-bacon was done, he put the strips on a paper towel to drain, and cooked himself two eggs in the same skillet. He plated his breakfast and sat at the table to eat. He sat directly across from me and watched me as he ate, slowly, seeming to enjoy every bite, like you would slowly sip a fine wine. After watching him eat the first couple of bites I stared at the floor and tried to think about something else." The attorney gagged. I looked at him. He was actually turning a sickening shade of green. "He...ate her?" he asked. I nodded. "That's so... so..." he said and gagged again. "Wrong?" "Yes," he exclaimed. "How did you get away?" I smiled gently and continued with my story. "Uncle Troy sat and ate every bite of his breakfast—chewing and watching me the whole time. The look in his eyes gave me chills. I saw him watching my breasts as I tried to breathe and yet not move because of the rope. I closed my eyes so I wouldn't see him watching me. But it was almost worse somehow, because with my eyes closed all I could do was smell and hear. I could smell the aroma of what he'd cooked and I heard his fork clink off the plate as he took each bite.

"Eventually the clinking stopped. I opened my eyes as I heard the scraping of a kitchen chair on the hardwood floor. I watched as Uncle Troy took his plate to the sink and washed it, as well as the other dishes he'd dirtied. He dried them and put them away. "He walked over beside me and began stroking my hair. Leaning down, he kissed my forehead. 'I'll be right back for you,' he said and went outside again. He went to the barn. At least that was the direction I saw him go. When he reappeared in my line of vision through the window, I saw a silver metal bucket in his hand; he was heading for the pig pens. "My mind was working a mile a minute, but I still couldn't think of a way to escape. I prayed again—for God to help me out of the mess I was in. I was just finishing my plea when I saw Uncle Troy again. He had mud smeared on his shirt and hands. The bucket was half-covered with mud as well. I remember thinking, Mud? Why mud? I didn't have to wait long to find out. "His boots thudded slowly on the porch; the screen door screeched as it opened. He stood there, in the doorway, staring at me for what felt like hours. I stared back, which seemed to excite him. He grinned and advanced into the room, walking around the table and over to where I sat. The bucket made a loud thunk as he sat it on the floor beside my chair. He knelt down in front of me and placed his hands on my knees, making me jump. He laughed. "He squeezed my legs. I'd never realized he was so big—I'd never been so close to him before. One of his hands was big enough to cover my knee and half of my thigh. He didn't say anything for the longest time. He just kept squeezing and rubbing my legs, his breath coming faster and faster. I was trembling, not only from fear, but from the continued strain of my physical position. It had to have been over an hour since he'd tied me to the chair. "Finally, he said, 'I'm gonna play nice with you, my sweet little piggy.' He dipped one of his hands into the bucket, and scooped out a big handful of mud. At least I hoped it was mud, my nose had been burning ever since he'd made his breakfast and I could no longer smell anything. He rubbed his hands together, caking them both with the thick brown slime. He put his hands back on my legs and began to smear the filth from my knees to the edge of my shorts. I felt his fingers slip further and further under them each time. I was crying uncontrollably. Sobs racked my body and I felt the rope tightening. I didn't care anymore. I just wanted it to be over. "At some point he must have decided my legs were brown enough, because he stopped. He moved around to the back of the chair and stood behind me. I could feel his breath against my neck as he bent toward me. He stuck out his tongue and licked from the base of my neck up to my ear. I gagged, jerking on the rope. "He laughed and loosened the rope to keep me alive. Bending over, he got more mud from the bucket and started to massage it into my shoulders and around my neck, getting closer and closer to the neckline of my shirt. 'Squeal like a piggy for me, honey,' he breathed in my ear. I jerked my head sideways and the rope tightened again. This time he didn't loosen it right away, but let me sputter and gag as he shoved his muddy hands down the front of my shirt. I started to black out and was thanking God for taking that much mercy on me, when he loosened the rope again.

"At that moment a truck pulled up in front of the house, drawing his attention to the living room windows. He swore and walked over to see who was there. I heard a truck door slam and heard him swear again. He turned, heading back toward me, passing by the stove. His boots were muddy and he slid in a bit of the grease he'd spilled earlier. Grabbing a chair, he righted himself, grinning. 'I'll be right back, my little piglet, to finish taking care of you,' he said. I cringed. "He'd turned to go outside when he slipped again, going down this time. Both of his muddy, booted feet flew up, hitting the underside of the kitchen table. He twisted in the air and his right temple hit the corner of the stove with a sickening crunch. He fell to the floor and didn't move." Closing my eyes, I took a deep breath. "Was he dead?" the attorney asked. "When he hit his head, did it kill him?" I nodded as tears slid down my cheeks. "A neighbor from the next farm over had come by to see if Uncle Troy had a part for his tractor. Uncle Troy and the neighbor had the same model and Uncle Troy had a couple of junk ones he kept for parts. When the neighbor didn't find Uncle Troy in the barn, he headed for the house. He spotted my aunt hanging on the porch and came running. He ran in the back door and saw Uncle Troy on the floor, and me, tied and gagged with mud all over me. He untied me and removed the gag. He ran to the phone and called 9-1-1. He kept saying, 'Oh Gawd, Oh Lordie, Oh Gawd.' "By the time he untied me—after making the call—I'd passed out. I don't know if it was from exhaustion, relief, or trauma. It took me two weeks before I was able to tell the sheriff what happened." "Wow, that's terrible," the attorney said. "Two people dead and for what? Burnt bacon?" I laughed harshly. "Yeah, burnt bacon. What a world, huh?" The attorney sat there for a moment, shaking his head, trying to wrap his mind around something no sane human could ever understand. "I don't get it though," he said frowning. "What does that have to do with you being here now?" I sighed. "I was engaged to Mark, which was great. We were in love and he was considerate and romantic. A week before we were to be married, he told me his favorite food was bacon and he would like to have it every morning for breakfast. I was stunned. He went on to tell me how he would like it to be cooked and that I better not burn it or I'd be punished. He laughed. If I'd thought about it for a moment, I would have known he was joking, or at least I'd like to think I would have known. But it was too late —I snapped. "I walked into the kitchen and took out the biggest, sharpest knife we owned. I came back to the living room and stabbed him. I don't remember how many times. All I could think about was that day at the farm when Uncle Troy killed my aunt and was about to rape me, all because of bacon. I guess I just lost it." I pushed my hands into my hair, resting my forehead on my palms. "Jesus," the attorney whispered. "You killed him because he liked bacon? Because of your uncle and how he snapped because of bacon? This is almost too ludicrous! I've never had such a case before! Are you pulling my leg? Because I really don't have time to be sent on a wild goose chase right now.

I have a huge case load." Dropping my hands, I looked at him with tears in my eyes. "I knew you wouldn't believe me," I accused. "You want proof? Call this sheriff." Grabbing his pen and a piece of his paper, I wrote down the name of the town and the sheriff who investigated the farm incident. He took the piece of paper, read it and reread it, then looked at me and blinked. "I'll look into it," he said, stuffing his files and papers back into his leather briefcase. "If this is all true, we have a good chance of pleading temporary insanity." I just sat there watching him. He was almost comical in his rush to get out of the cell. "I'll be in touch," he said over his shoulder as he dashed out the door. I saw him lean toward the guard standing just far enough down the corridor not to hear our conversation. I didn't catch all he said, but I heard the word bacon echo down the hall. I threw my head back and laughed about the absurdity of it all. The death count was rising. Three dead on account of bacon.

A Day at the Morgue by Anthony Giangregorio

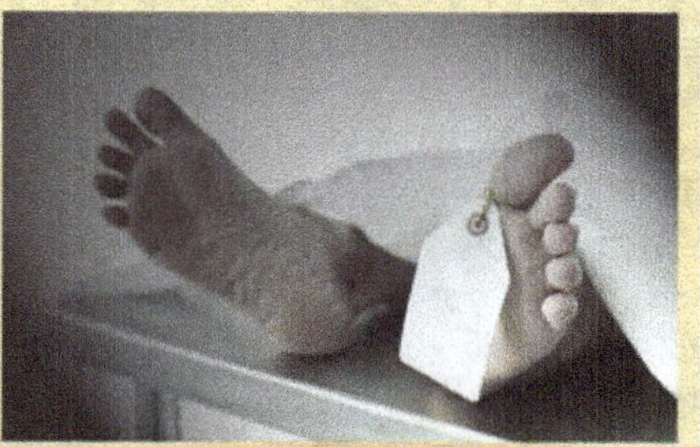

"Got another one for you, Doug," the orderly said as he wheeled yet another body into the morgue of the Belham Hospital. Doug turned around and frowned deeply. "Oh, come on, Roger, really? I've got them stacked two to a table as it is." "Not my problem," Roger replied as he handed Doug a clipboard so he could sign off on the body. Doug took the clipboard and scrawled his name at the bottom. "I just don't know what the city expects me to do around here. It's only me and Bob now thanks to cutbacks and layoffs." Roger shrugged. "Hey, man, it's tough all over." With a casual wave that said he wasn't interested in Doug's problems, he left leaving Doug standing with yet another body. Doug sighed as he stared down at the corpse in the black body bag. "Now where the hell am I supposed to put you?" As he looked around the large room, he really didn't have an answer to his question. There were more than thirty bodies in the morgue at the moment, more than half of them thanks to a bus crash out on Interstate 95. No survivors, he'd been told. A drunk driver had cut off the bus and it had gone through the guardrail and into a twenty foot ravine. Many of the corpses were in pieces while others had no more than bruises, their deaths due to internal bleeding. It had been a horror show. At least there had been no children involved, Doug figured, as it was a bus heading off to the gambling casino in the next state. He had a stack of autopsies to do and now he had another to add to the list. He looked up as Bob walked in, holding a sandwich. He was still wearing his apron, a splash of mustard in the middle of his chest. "Hey, what's up? Another one?" he asked around a mouthful of pastrami on rye with extra mustard. "Yeah, another one. I swear, the city's gonna kill me. Give it another week and I'm gonna be on a slab next to the rest of these poor bastards." Bob said nothing, merely continued chomping on his sandwich. Doug wasn't please with this. "Tell me, Bob, how would you feel about cutting me open if I was dead and in here?" Bob shrugged. "A stiff is a stiff to me, Doug, you know that. If you ever ended up on my table, I'd do the same to you as the rest. Hey, it's my job." Doug couldn't refute the reasoning. "Yeah, I guess you're right." He sighed. "Okay, where are we gonna put this one?" Bob let out a burp and wiped his mouth with the back of his sleeve. His eyes scanned the room and the available space, which there was none. The best course of action would be to move a body and make that one next for an autopsy, then they could put the new arrival in its place. But Bob hated doing more work than was necessary, and he had an idea. "Hey, Doug, why don't we just get this stiff done now and then we don't have to play musical cadavers." Doug considered it and nodded.

"You know what? That's not a bad idea. For once your laziness is coming in handy." Bob gave Doug a mustard-covered middle finger in reply. "Yeah, I am number one," Doug snapped back, a grin on his face. "Now finish that damn sandwich and give me a hand. I swear, sometimes I have to wonder if you're the boss of me instead of the other way around, the way you act." "Ah, Doug, relax. I know you're in charge, I'm just messin' with you." Doug waited by the corpse for Bob to gobble down the rest of his sandwich. When he was finished, he walked over to the rolling gurney. "Ah, Bob, you got a little mustard on your face," Doug said and pointed to the very large splatter of mustard. It made Bob look like he had a yellow mustache. Bob never was one for food etiquette and Doug was usually glad when his friend at least chewed his food. Bob wiped his mouth with the back of his sleeve and belched again. Doug waved the air with his hand, trying to blow away the odor of regurgitated pastrami. "Damn, man, it tastes as good comin' back up as it did goin' down," Bob grinned, enjoying the fact that his supervisor was uncomfortable. "Just give me a hand here, will you please?" Bob did as he was asked and grabbed the feet of the corpse and Doug did the same to the head. He grabbed the body bag and then heaved it off the rolling gurney and onto a stainless steel table placed in the middle of the room. There was a microphone connected to a steel pole which was connected to the ceiling. Doug reached up and pressed the bottom on the side of the mic, and as he began to talk, he slid on a pair of new latex white gloves. "Okay, so we have yet another customer for my table." He unzipped the body bag and barely acknowledged the stench of death. As a coroner for over ten years, there wasn't much that could surprise him. "Bob, give me a hand sliding him out of the body bag, will you?" Doug asked. Bob helped roll the cadaver over, and as he held the body on its side, Doug slid the bag off like a night nurse changing the soiled sheets of an infirm patient. "Wow, this guy is really messed up," Bob said as he gazed down at the face of the cadaver. I wonder what happened to him." Doug picked up the small booklet that was attached to the body bag. It was a preliminary of what the paramedics had found upon discovering the body. "Says here," Doug began, "that the body was found in a ditch about ten miles outside the city under mysterious circumstances with no ID." He flipped through some of the pages. "Says here there was no foliage around the body. It was like the entire area had been blasted clean from fire, like scorched earth." "Cool, maybe this guy was probed and left behind by aliens." "What?" "You know," Bob said, "like crop circles and shit." Doug frowned. "Don't be an idiot." "What? I'm just sayin'. Hear me out. Guy in a ditch, dead, no living matter around him, looks like it was all burnt. I'm tellin' you, it's an alien dumpsite." "Like I said before, you're an idiot," Doug frowned. Bob gave Doug the one finger salute in reply and reached into his pocket and took out his cell phone.

As he checked his messages, Doug continued. "Caucasian male, bald with no discernable markings—scars or tattoos—appears to be late fifties or early sixties." He began undressing the man. "Appears to have bruising to right clavicle, but I'll know more when I perform the autopsy." He removed the body's shirt and said, "Oh, wait, revise what I said. Male has distinctive tattoo of what looks like a military insignia. My recommendations for the detective assigned to the case, is to check for military service if a fingerprint hit doesn't come up." He looked at Bob. "Put that damn thing away and take off his shoes, socks and pants, will you?" Bob slid his phone into a pocket as dexterous as a magician. Then he got to work. Moments later, the corpse was naked and pale in the harsh light of the room. Doug used a spotlight and aimed it at the torso of the corpse. "Hmm, this is odd," he said and Bob leaned forward to see better. "What's odd? "This." Doug pointed a latex-covered finger at the cadaver's belly button. "It looks like there's dried blood here, as if something had crawled into him through his belly button. He pulled down a large magnifying glass attached to another bendable pole that hung from the ceiling. Angling it just so, he and Bob studied the odd wound. "Maybe he got stabbed and it's a coincidence he got it in the belly button," Bob suggested. Doug turned his head and Bob's face was only inches from his. He smelled pastrami and sweat and neither was appetizing. "I highly doubt you're right but once more, guessing is irrelevant. We'll have all our answers when we open him up." Doug gestured to a tray of instruments on a small rolling table. "Bring that over here and I'll make the first incision." Bob pushed the small table over so Doug could reach the tray easily. Doug picked up a small, two inch scalpel, and without hesitation, sliced into the chest cavity of the cadaver from neck to groin. When he finished the incision, he put on a small face shield, picked up a bone saw, and began cutting at the ribcage. Thirty seconds later and he was holding the rib spreader as he cracked the chest cavity and exposed the organs to the harsh, unnatural light of the morgue. As he set the rib spreader down, he heard Bob utter a small noise, like a squeak. Not looking down at the corpse, he instead turned to Bob to ask him what was wrong. Bob was staring down at the vivisected corpse, his mouth hanging open in what appeared to be shock, surprise, horror, or both. Slowly, Doug turned away from Bob to look back down at the cadaver. When his eyes connected with the exposed torso, his mouth fell open and he stopped breathing, his pulse pounding in his temple. In the middle of the exposed chest cavity, covered in gore and slime, was what looked like an electric eel, only this one was thick as a grown man's forearm with two small arms, and a mouth filled with razor sharp teeth. Two yellow eyes blinked clear of the slime covering the head, and as Doug stared in shock, the mouth opened wide and hissed, a small tongue forking out, similar to a snake's only dark black. "What the fuck is that?" Bob squeaked as he fought the urge to scream.

"How the hell should I know?" Doug gasped in reply. "What do we do?" "I don't know, kill it, capture it, make it a pet and bring it home…shit, Bob, this is a little new to me. I don't know about you, but this is the first time I've cut into a corpse and had a friggin' snake pop out of it." "That ain't no snake." The eel hissed again, its small head moving back and forth, as if it wanted to look at each of the men at the same time but couldn't. The tongue continued to lick the air, and Doug wondered if it could somehow taste them, sense them in the same way a snake did. "Try and capture it," Bob said. "That's like no snake I've ever seen before. We could make a fortune showing the news it. Hell, maybe it's some kind of weird new species." Doug looked at Bob and then at the eel. "Fine, I'll try to catch it." He slowly sucked in a breath of air and then cautiously moved closer to the eel and the corpse beneath it, the body for all purposes looking like a gut-filled nest. When he was less than a foot away, the eel hissed and lunged for his face. "Look out!" Bob yelled as Doug snapped his head back, the eel whistling by his face by less than an inch. As it passed his face, the tail slapped his nose and left a bit of slime there. He felt the patch of skin begin to burn. He quickly wiped it off and the burning ceased. "Get it! Get it!" Bob yelled as the eel landed on the floor and slid as if it was on ice. "You fucking get it!" Doug yelled back. Now that it was free of the corpse, the two men could now see the bottom of the eel. It had legs as well as arms. Rolling to its tiny feet, it began to run away from them. "It's getting away!" Bob yelled. "No shit, go catch it!" Bob spun and picked up a specimen pan, the four inch deep, one foot round bowl something good to use as a cage in a pinch. With bowl in hand, he turned and dashed after the eel. At the same time it ran under one of the other gurneys with a corpse on it. Bob was so focused on the eel that he crashed into the corpse and knocked it and the gurney over. The body crashed to the floor with a dull thump, the table making much more noise as steel collided with cement. Bob had fallen, too, and was now lying on the corpse. The body, having Bob on it and becoming condensed such as when you squeeze a balloon, began to release trapped gas. The sound of farts of all kinds, long ones, short ones and trumpeting ones, all exploded out of the corpse's anus, filling the room with a miasma that had both men gagging. Bob rolled off the corpse and the farting ceased, and for a moment he lost sight of the eel. Then he turned around and looked behind him and saw it staring at him. "What the hell is it doing…" he began and then the eel began to run at him. When it was three feet away, it jumped into the air, flying directly at Bob's face. Acting fast, he used the bowl as a shield, and with a metallic clang, the eel bounced off it and rolled onto the floor. But it was up in a second and it ran around Bob and right at the corpse. Bob tried to use the bowl to capture it but missed, and the eel skated out of his grasp. Then it turned and dashed for the fallen corpse again. Bob could only watch in amazement as it ran at the cadaver, and then like it was covered in Vaseline, the head went into the corpse's mouth and the rest soon followed.

Like sucking in spaghetti, the eel had slithered into the head of the corpse and only a slime trail around the lips showed it had ever been there. "What the fuck?" Bob gasped as Doug came over to him, his eyes looking left and right for the eel. "Where did it go?" Doug asked. Bob pointed to the head of the corpse. "In there." "In where?" Doug was wondering if his friend had cracked under the pressure. "In there, in the fucking body, the thing just slithered into its mouth and disappeared." "Bullshit," Doug snapped. "That's impossible." "No it's not, Doug. Are you calling me a fucking liar?" "No I... I mean to say I..." He took a deep breath to calm himself. "Okay, let's not fight, that won't accomplish anything." He leaned down and grabbed the arms of the corpse. "Get the legs and let's get this cadaver back on the slab." Bob stood up and righted the gurney, then he picked up the legs. They both lifted and the body was soon on the slab once more. The cadaver was a woman, looking as if she had died in her late sixties or early seventies. The scar of a pacemaker showed she'd had a bad heart and was the reason for her internment in the morgue. Doug went to the head of the dead woman and began to examine her mouth, touching his finger to the slime. He raised it to his nose and sniffed, then winced and quickly wiped it off on his apron. "God, that smells horrible, and believe me, I've smelled some terrible stuff in my career." "So what do we do now? It's in the body. Are we gonna leave it there?" Bob asked. Doug shook his head. "No, no way. This is Mrs. Wilson. She's got a date with the grave tomorrow at the funeral home and her family is very wealthy. I don't want them suing me for negligence or whatever when I ship her over to the funeral parlor. No, we need to get it out of her. I can fix her up with some glue when we're done if I have to and the mortician is a friend of mine. If I ask for a favor, he'll help me out. One hand washes the other and all that. Besides, she's having a closed casket anyway. Hell, we could bury a couple of bags of cement and no one would probably ever know." "Then why don't we do that instead?" "What did I just say? If we tried it and the family found out, they'd sue me into bankruptcy. You know the city wouldn't defend me, not with the budget crisis. I'd be living in a cardboard box by the end of the year." As Doug talked, neither man was looking down at Mrs. Wilson, so they didn't see the fingers on her left hand begin to twitch. "So get cuttin', man, get it out of there," Bob said and was about to say more when he glanced down at the body to see the hand squeeze into a fist. "Oh my God, no fucking way," he whispered and took a step back. "What? What now? Bob, you need to keep it together if we're gonna do what needs to be done here." Bob didn't reply, but instead pointed down at the body. Doug slowly followed where Bob was gesturing and his mouth fell open when he saw Mrs. Wilson's hand in a fist, then her other hand rising up. "But...this is impossible, she's been embalmed," he said in utter disbelief. "She can't be moving. It's physically impossible." "Well, shit, Doug, maybe someone didn't bother to tell her that," Bob said as he stumbled into a gurney behind him.

The body on the gurney began to waver, as if it wasn't sure if it was going to fall, then the gurney tilted that extra inch and toppled. It hit the gurney next to it, and like dominoes, ten bodies and gurneys all dropped on the floor in a splaying of arms, legs and crashing tables, all the corpses as naked as the day they were born. Bob dropped into the pile between three of the bodies, and as arms fell on him, he began to yell, totally freaked out. Then he felt hands on him and yelled yet again, knowing it had to be one of the corpses, that the body had revived and was trying to kill him. But it was only Doug, who had run to him to help him up. "Oh shit, it's only you," Bob gasped as he was helped to his feet. Then he looked over Doug's shoulder to see Mrs. Wilson was now sitting up and her dead eyes were glaring right at him. "Holy shit," Bob whispered. "She's fucking alive." Also naked, as she hadn't been dressed for her funeral yet, and her pale skin seemed to absorb the yellow light of the overhead fluorescent lights. As she slowly slid off the gurney, her skin undulated, as if a hundred worms were beneath her skin. "No, Bob, I don't think she's actually alive. I think whatever that snake thing is, it's inside her and somehow controlling her." "So she's a fucking zombie?" "No, I wouldn't say that, but it's a fair description for now." Mrs. Wilson was staring at the two men, and ever so slowly, she reached out to the small table with the instruments on it. Ever so carefully, her fingers touched a scalpel, and she gripped it tightly, a sinister smile crossing her pale lips. Then she opened her mouth and hissed, one very similar to the eel when it had burst forth from the cadaver. Both men were frozen in shock, the unbelievable too much for them to handle. The eel was one thing, that at least was something they could relate to as it looked similar to a large snake, but this, an embalmed woman now standing, grasping a scalpel and actually smiling was over the top. The entire time she grasped the tool, her skin flexed and rippled, like an endless ocean was just under her withered flesh. "What the hell do we do?" Bob whispered to Doug, who only shook his head. "I have no idea," he replied. Before either man could act, the old woman was upon them, moving way too fast for a corpse. The scalpel in her hand was like a living thing, rising and falling as the two men tried to fend her off. But skin and bone was no a match for steel, and razor-sharp surgical steel at that. As hands were raised to block the blows, fingers were slashed off and wrists were sliced to let arteries flow freely. Mrs. Wilson's left arm was broken in two places when Doug tried to attack her, but a slice to his throat stopped him cold. As he fell to the floor, his life's blood draining out of his severed carotid artery to pool around him, she continued to rain blows down on Bob. As Doug bled out on the floor, Bob valiantly tried to save his own life. His arms were slashed a dozen times and his clothes were slick with blood from the multiple slashes. He knew he needed to escape or he would join Doug on the floor, covered in blood. Taking a chance, he kicked out with his right leg, and though he received a slash to his knee, he managed to kick Mrs. Wilson in her left knee. The shattering of the frail knee cap filled the room and Mrs. Wilson toppled over to break a hip.

She had fallen and she couldn't get up. Bob ran to the left, where shelves of chemicals were stored. One of the chemicals was hydrochloric acid. Breathing heavily, the plastic jar slippery from his blood, he barely managed to open it as Mrs Wilson began to crawl toward him, her teeth flashing in the light of the room, her dead eyes looking as if cataracts had completely enveloped them. How she could see, Bob had no idea. When she was within a few feet of him, she tried to slash his legs and he jumped back, uttering a small scream. Behind her, he could see Doug was still, his dead eyes gazing up at the ceiling. Bob shook his head, trying to stay sane, even if for just a little longer. He wondered if perhaps this was all a dream and he would wake up in his bed covered in sweat but safe. Hissing snapped him from his wish as Mrs. Wilson came closer. With acid in hand, he stepped forward and then to the side when she slashed at him. He dumped the acid on her head and back, then jumped away fast. A few drops got on him and he felt the sting as the acid ate through his clothing and into his skin. But they were small and only the top two layers of skin were eaten before the acid stopped working. Mrs. Wilson was spasming and twitching, a hideous scream leaving her pale lips. The acid ate away her hair, skin and the meat on her bones, the bubbling soup spreading out around her. Soon, her face was nothing but a grinning skull, and as Bob watched, the tongue boiled and disintegrated, the foul liquid splashing in the goop that was her body, her eyes soon following as they literally dissolved and dripped out of her eye sockets. The arm with the scalpel tried to reach for him but with half her body eaten away, there was no way she could accomplish her goal. Then the acid ate enough that whatever the eel was using to control her ceased and the corpse slumped to the floor, splashing gore in all directions. Steam and bubbles rose from the body as the acid continued to dissolve her. Bob breathed a sigh of relief, and without checking on Doug—or Mrs. Wilson—he turned, and after giving the bubbling body a wide berth, he ran for the exit and freedom. As he ran down the hall, he screamed for help; about alien snakes, walking corpses and murder. As the door slammed closed and the sound of Bob's yelling and footsteps pounding down the hallway ceased, the morgue grew silent. Then, a scraping sound could be heard, and under Mrs. Wilson's right leg, the eel popped free of a new hole it had made in the corpse's thigh. It had burrowed into the leg when the acid began to work and had survived unscathed. Popping free, it ran across the floor and right to Doug. After sniffing at the blood with its tongue, it scampered into the crimson pool and onto Doug's chest. The tongue licked out once more and then the eel slid up to the jagged slash in Doug's neck. In the blink of an eye, it crawled into the gaping wound and into his body. Like he was swallowing something really large, Doug's throat undulated, then went still once more. For a few seconds nothing happened and all was quiet in the morgue, with the exception of the bubbling corpse of Mrs. Wilson as the acid continued to eat away at her flesh and bones.

Doug's blank eyes were open and staring at nothing and then they blinked. His mouth moved as did his hands, and a minute later he was sitting up. He moved his head from side to side, blood seeping from the wound, and when he had composed himself, so to speak, he slowly picked himself up to a standing position. He swayed back and forth for a few seconds as he regained his balance, then walked over to a small supply closet. Inside was the clothing of the deceased that came through the morgue. Jackets, shirts, pants, socks and sometimes underwear; but not too often. The latter was usually cut away and disposed of, given the predilection for the diseased to defecate upon death. This was where it was all stored until being taken away monthly. Doug slowly stripped off his bloody clothes, and as he did, his wounds began to stop bleeding. With no beating heart there was nothing to pump the blood and most of it was now on the floor anyway. He carefully wiped himself down, especially his arms, legs and face, then he took a scarf and tied it around his neck to cover his wound. After putting on a new pair of shoes, he shrugged into a Red Sox jacket and put on a Yankees ball cap, having no idea the two together were a taboo. After flexing his arms and legs and bending his head back and forth one more time to make sure everything worked the way it was supposed to, he walked out of the morgue. When he exited, he went in the opposite direction that Bob had taken. The morgue fell quiet once more, only the bubbling of Mrs. Wilson to break the silence.

"Planet of the Vampires" Reviewed by Tony Schaab

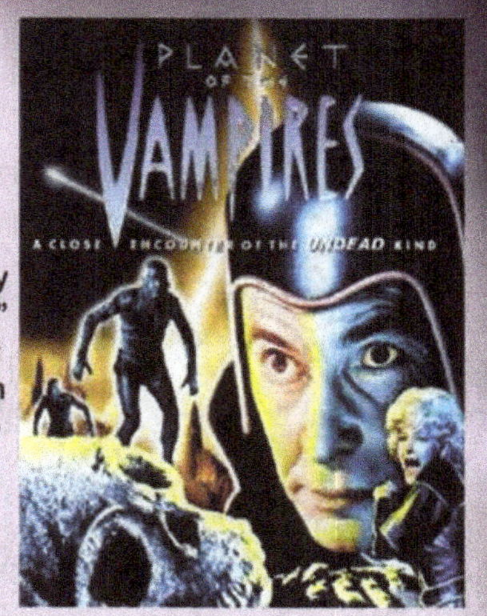

There are many great horror movies out there that you simply don't know about. Sure, everyone is familiar with "A Nightmare on Elm Street," "Friday the 13th," "The Blair Witch Project," and the like, but what about the movies that might not have been as big of a commercial success but should still be considered some of the genre's finest work? The purpose of this and other reviews in this magazine is to introduce you to these hidden gems, so you can learn more about them, seek them out and watch them, and elevate yourself to "true horror fan" status. At first glance, "Planet of the Vampires" could easily be mistaken for just another kitschy '60s sci-fi B-movie. But those "in the know" revere this movie as one of the first crossover horror/sci-fi films, a front-runner for great movies like "Alien" and "Event Horizon." Filmed at Cinecittà Studios in Rome, the movie features an international cast, and was shot by director Mario Bava on a shoestring budget–but Bava did such a great job of making the film look like a big production that you definitely wouldn't think otherwise while watching it. In the film, two large interplanetary exploration ships, the Argos and the Galliott, respond to a distress signal originating from the unexplored planet Aura. Upon their attempts to land, both crews become possessed by an unknown force and violently try to kill each other; only through the willpower and efforts of Captain Mark Markay, commander of the Argos, is the Argos' crew prevented from seriously injuring each other. Upon traversing the treacherous molten terrain of the planet to reach the now-unresponsive Galliott, Argos' crew discovers that their comrades on the other ship were not as fortunate as they were; they lay strewn about the ship, apparently murdered by one another. The unknown forces that originally possessed the Argos' crew return, but instead of occupying the living survivors, the forces inhabit the bodies of the dead crew members, reanimating them from their hastily-constructed graves. While fending off the reanimated creatures and trying to fix the Argos so they can escape, Markay and the survivors come across a crashed alien ship housing huge skeletal remains of other aliens. The crew knows their situation is dire, and they are in a race against the clock to escape the force that has inhabited the bodies of their dead comrades. In a thrilling climax, much is revealed about the true nature of the unknown force, and the movie boasts not one but two inspired plot twists at the conclusion of the film that I never saw coming! The creation of the film itself has some amazing stories as well. The production was so pressed for time, the actors–who all came from a variety of international backgrounds–all spoke their lines in their native languages (including English, Portuguese, Italian, and Spanish), often times having no idea what the other actors were saying! This helps to explain the nagging sensation the viewer will encounter when it seems that some actors' lines are dubbed into English, causing a disconnect between the actors' mouth movements and what they are heard to be saying, while others appear in perfect synchronization. Since the film was so groundbreaking for its time, the studio really had no idea what to name it. The original Italian title of the film, "Terrore Nello Spazio," translates to "Terror in Space." Other titles attached to the movie in its various stages of pre-and post-production included: "Planet of Blood," "Space Mutants," "The Demon Planet," "The Haunted Planet," "The Outlawed Planet," "The Planet of Terror," and "The Planet of the Damned." The confusion/indecision in naming the movie most likely came from the fact that the type of creatures portrayed in the film–reanimated humans possessed by an unknown force–had really never been clearly defined before this movie was released. Even though the film's title is "Planet of the Vampires," the beings portrayed here are actually closer to zombies, but this film was released in 1965, three years before George Romero's "Night of the Living Dead" would adequately characterize the genre for us. As previously mentioned, the film was shot entirely working under a very minimalistic budget; it already looked remarkable (for its time), but Bava's finished product is even more impressive with this knowledge. Extensive use of miniatures and "forced perspectives" are used in the film, including tons of colored fog on the planet's surface to help hide the fact that they were actually just shooting on a bare-bones set. In an interview with Tim Lucas, Bava expounded on the process: "Do you know what that unknown planet was made of? A couple of plastic rocks —yes, two: one and one!—left over from a mythological movie made at Cinecittà! To assist the illusion, I filled the set with smoke." According to Lucas, the two plastic rocks were multiplied in several shots by mirrors and multiple exposures. One scene that Bava didn't want to skimp on, however, was the sequence where Markay and two other crew members encountered a derelict alien spaceship. As the astronauts clambered around the large ship, they discovered multiple skeletal remains of gigantic, long-dead alien life forms. This scene draws immediate comparisons to the extended "space jockey" scene in Ridley Scott's film "Alien," and rightfully so: produced fourteen years after "Planet of the Vampires," Scott's scene has a great deal of similarity to and evokes much of the same feel as the one presented in this movie. Upon "Alien's" release in 1979, the horror magazine Cinefantastique ran an article pointing out not only this obvious similarity, but other minor parallels between the two films. Both director Scott and screenwriter Dan O'Bannon claimed at the time that they had never seen "Planet of the Vampires." Even without all of this fun background knowledge of the movie, "Planet of the Vampires" is an incredibly rich story and a great viewing experience that has withstood the test of time and can easily entertain the "true horror fan" of today. I highly recommend you seek this movie out and give it a watch; you won't be disappointed.

The Lost Continent

Hammer Film Productions is an iconic film production company. Based in the United Kingdom, the company was founded in 1934, and is probably best known for its series of "Hammer Horror" films it produced from the mid-1950s through the late 1960s. From 1950 until 1969, the company produced a whopping 147 different feature-length movies. Hammer's most popular films are names you're most likely familiar with: "Frankenstein," "Dracula," "The Mummy" (along with their various sequels), "One Million Years B.C.," and "The Phantom of the Opera." But the company also has a plethora of other great horror films that probably aren't on your radar. Among these is the trippy, kitschy movie-watching experience that is 1968's "The Lost Continent." "The Lost Continent" is one of the first films to effectively use the "ending as the opening" gimmick, where the final chronological scene of the story is actually used as the opening shot of the film. Immediately following the ultra-'60s opening credits, replete with popular British band The Peddlers crooning the title-tracked theme song, we're introduced to the crew and passengers of the dilapidated cargo ship Corita, as they gather on deck to witness Captain Lansen presiding over a burial at sea. As the camera pans across, we're introduced to a group of characters that seemed to have gathered for an ocean cruise across the borders of time: hooded priests, pirates, Spanish conquistadores, seamen, and beautiful women are all present on deck to witness the funeral rites. As the body is pitched overboard, Lansen's internal dialogue wonders "What happened to us? How did we all get here?" The screen gets wavy in the classic "flashback" form, and the viewer is whisked back in time to the start of the tale. To go too far into detail on the finer points of the convoluted plot line would be to ruin the movie-watching experience for the uninitiated viewer, but suffice it to say that the Corita's journey is indeed a long and strange one. The ship leaves port in Freetown, South Africa in quite the hurry, much to the relief of both Captain Lansen and his motley assortment of passengers, each seemingly with their own shady reasons for traveling on this subpar vessel rather than a standard passenger ship. Since they're purposefully avoiding all the major shipping and commercial travel lanes, it isn't long before the ship finds itself off-course (an impending hurricane does little to help matters). Through a series of haphazard events, passengers and crew are forced to abandon ship, but their lifeboats oddly returning them to the still-intact Corita is just the beginning of the strange events that are to follow. They soon become mired in a murky sea amidst a graveyard of ships, and the characters engage in a series of encounters each more fantastic than the last, including giant octopi, seaweed with a mind of its own, marauders wearing strange shoes and lighter-than-air balloon harnesses on their shoulders, descendants of the Spanish Inquisition, and even giant, rocky crustaceans fighting each other. The tale concludes in a maddeningly open-ended fashion that will leave viewers wondering far after the credits roll. The film initially began under the direction of Leslie Norman, but for reasons unknown he was quickly replaced by Michael Carreras, the son of Hammer's founder, James Carreras. The younger Carreras directed a total of nine Hammer films, including what is largely believed to be the first Spaghetti-Western ever produced, "The Savage Guns." Eagle-eyed viewers of "The Lost Continent" will notice that the screenplay was written by "Michael Nash," which is actually one of Carreras' pseudonyms; why he chose to use an alternate name in the credits is anyone's guess! Since much of the shoot took place on the boat, with exterior shots showing the seascape that it necessitated, a very specific type of set was built for the movie. A huge tank was constructed at the fame Elstree Studios in England. Holding a whopping 175,000 gallons of water, the tank held the Corita life-size set as well as some of the other boat and island settings that appear in the movie. This may not sound like a terribly impressive feat now in the days of CGI, but back in the mid-1960s, this was quite an impressive investment into a horror film. Fortunately, Hammer was able to make many of their movies profitable, and "The Lost Continent" was such a unique viewing experience that viewers have kept it alive as a cult favorite to this day. The combination of unique plot (even if it is difficult to follow at times), eclectic characters, and a healthy mix of fantastic elements that don't immediately seem to go together but somehow do, all make for a one-of-a-kind film that, quite simply, has to be seen to be believed and appreciated. "The Lost Continent" is available on DVD, allowing the audience of the digital age to enjoy this truly distinctive movie.

DO UNTO OTHERS: BY DANE T. HATCHELL

Nick Ott wanted to shut his eyes and blank out the image of the room and the implements used to inflict his suffering. Not that closing his eyes would do anything to quench the pain. He was grasping for some type of relief from the excruciating agony his entire body had been enduring for an undeterminable length of time. His anguish was so intense that he couldn't remember a time when he wasn't being tortured. The constant abuse kept his mind impaled to each succeeding second. He hoped if he could just close his eyes that somehow he could recall memories of more pleasant times, or create a fantasy that offered some respite. Anything to somehow distract himself by blocking out the images of the ghastly devices being used on him like a corpse on an autopsy table. Never could he imagine the sheer amount of pain that the body could feel. He was in horrid wonder of the creative methods of his torture. Such ingenuity, as one area of nerves was overloaded to the point of being numb, another would be targeted. Always fresh, always unique. Nick thought about death, the various ways to die that he used to be fearful of. Drowning had always terrified him, and the thought of not being able to breathe broke him out in a cold sweat. Burning at the stake would engage every pain nerve in the body, and he had feared death by fire the worst. However, the pain the blow torch brought to his genitals as they were roasted to a black crisp lasted longer than if his entire body had been doused in gasoline and set on fire. How he wished his entire body had been set aflame then; his life would be over now. There was nothing that had prepared Nick for his predicament. Events such as these happened in ancient times, or by ruthless foreign military regimes. The portrayals of sadist capturing and torturing people were nothing more than fictitious creations of authors and movie directors to scare and entertain people. Dark minds defiling the innocent, causing them to imagine the unimaginable. What demented mind thinks like this? he wondered. His body felt fresh waves of pain to each part of him as his mind uncontrollably recalled the abuse he endured.
The knife used to split his tongue in half was dull and chipped. He'd felt the cold blade as it traveled every individual millimeter, the tongue being loaded with pain receptor nerves. Blood mixed with saliva had drooled down his chin, dripping down to the floor like unholy rain. Through the haze of shock, he wasn't able to identify the next tool his abuser chose from the table. It was an odd device that resembled a pear with a long threaded screw on the end. Nick winced in anticipation of being bludgeoned by it. Instead, his torturer walked behind him, and he heard a sound like liquid being squirted from a bottle.

He was unprepared as the pear was shoved deep into his rectum, and burning pain shot through his groin area. If the sodomy alone had not been severe enough, the screw was turned and the outside halves of the pear widened. The pain grew exponentially, until he felt his bowels were pushing on his throat. Nick had heard of death by one thousand cuts, and he wished so badly it was true. His captor used a box cutter with the barest of the blade exposed, to make tiny cuts over his entire body. Surely the man had cut him a thousand times ten. Every cut was a sharp annoying pain, fresh each slice, over and over again, until it felt like an army of fire ants was consuming him one bit of flesh at a time. There were other things done to him. With hammers, with saws, clamping tools, and pointed objects of every variety. Toes crushed, soft tissue mashed, cuts as deep as bone itself. His captor was thorough, ensuring that each individual fingernail on both hands had its own four inch bamboo sliver shoved underneath. Nick's throat was sore from the constant screaming and so dry that if given the chance, he would have cut his wrist in order to drink his own blood to quench his thirst, and invited the darkness of death to comfort him at the same time. His torturer had told him the reason for his unfortunate fate, but he could no longer remember. The cruel man now sat across the room, his elbows propped on the arms of an ornate mahogany chair, while enjoying a cigarette. The stale smoke mixed with the metallic smell of blood and the pheromones of fear. As Nick hung by his arms from chains connected to the ceiling, he tried to speak, to beg the man again for mercy. Whether that mercy came in the form of letting him go or swiftly ending his life, he didn't care anymore, and he hadn't cared for a long time if he lived or died. He only wanted relief. His torturer stood from the chair and adjusted the arms of his dark suit. He walked to the table of implements and chose what Nick thought was a pair of pliers. He was mistaken. His torturer seemed refreshed, and eager to get back to work. With the fish skinners in hand, he maliciously peeled the skin off Nick's entire body, starting at his face. Most strips were small, the tiny cuts having weakened the tension of skin. As the skin was peeled off, the man dusted the exposed dermis with table salt. It added to the pain, and minimized the much needed blood to preserve consciousness. With his laborious task complete, the man stepped back to admire his new creation. He was very pleased. A full length mirror in its stand, ornamented with chrome knobs, faced the wall next to the chair. The torturer carefully retrieved it, and moved it in front of his victim. Moving his body in front of the mirror, he positioned it so that a hanging Nick would see the masterful artwork he had created. He stepped away. Nick saw the image, and his mind at first couldn't grasp that the reflection was of a human being, much less that he was looking at himself.

It appeared more like an alien from another world with its insides turned out. Despite all the horrors that he had experienced, the image reached a hidden part in his mind, and snapped the last bit of sanity remaining. Sounds of hoarse laughter gurgled from Nick's throat as he twisted his body with newfound strength. Realizing that his victim was beyond the threshold of pain, the torturer made two incisions in Nick's abdomen with a surgical knife. The intestines fell to the floor in a bloody mess. The man tied the large intestine around Nick's neck, and removed one of the chains from around his wrist. Tying the intestine to the free chain, he then pushed a button on the wall which lifted the chain, and tightened the intestine around Nick's neck, cutting the air from his lungs completely, and finally giving the man the sweet release of death. "Hey, handsome, looking for a date?" the small-framed girl asked, after the sound of her six inch heels clomping on the pavement came to an abrupt halt. A thin-faced man stood in front of the facade of a poorly lit jewelry store. His black derby shadowed his eyes, but did nothing to conceal either his large nose or the festering sore on its tip. He made no attempt to look in the direction of the girl's voice. Even in the night, the paleness of the girl's skin was evident. Skin that hadn't seen daylight for months, if not years. Her deep purple blouse plunged at the neckline, revealing flat, sagging breasts and the outline of her ribcage. She chewed gum in rhythm to her heart beat, shifted her weight to her left knee, twirled her jet black hair with a thin finger, and waited for an answer. The man was as motionless as a mannequin. He was dressed in a black wool suit with perfect fit and fine detail. The two-button jacket sported thin lapels, four-button cuffs, and front flap welt pockets. A match exploded in yellow flame directly in front of his face and was cast aside to the ground after lighting the cigarette. He took a long drag from the cancer stick, and offered the girl one from the pack held in his other hand. She took the cigarette without a word, pulled a lighter from the side of her handbag, and set it burning. Taking a puff, she asked, "You want to go down the alley or back to a room?" The man tilted his head back and their eyes met. Finally revealed, his gaunt face and thin mustache made her left eye twitch in repulsion. The man's eyes widened, the frozen features on his face contorting in animation. "My child, it's a dark and dreary night. A time of night not fit for men of respect or women of virtue. Has life not offered you many paths? Isn't the world teaming with opportunity? How is it that you've become a random piece of debris floating down a river of human sewage?" An unusual feeling overtook her, and cold fear laced its damp tentacles around her insides. Her mind told her to run, but her legs were somehow paralyzed by the mysterious man's presence. An engulfing power surrounded her, and penetrated her mind. It was if he was looking inside her, reading all of her hidden sins. "Speak, girl," was all he said. Like a repentant child, she opened up to him.

"I've been scared all my life. I've been afraid that no one loves me. Not my parents, not my friends, no one. I was a burden to my parents as a child. My father never wanted me, and my mother resented me because of it. I was always in the way, always a wedge between them and the other things they wanted in life." She paused as tears trickled down her face and dripped off her chin. "But I tried. Really, I tried to get them to love me. I listened to them, I did everything they wanted me to do to get them to love me. But it was never enough." She stopped as her tears turned to sobs. She wiped the tears from her face with her hand and sniffed back snot building in her nostrils, took another puff from her cigarette, and composed herself. "I tried to win friends, but all they did was take advantage of me. I tried to get men to love me, but all they did was use me and throw me away. I have no one." She paused again. "No one! Do you hear me? No one!" "Yet I find you here on the street. You're certainly with purpose now. You're no longer alone, are you?" he asked. "No…not since I met Raoul." She lowered her head and grimaced a bitter smile. "I arrived in this town by bus with nothing. He took me in and took care of me." The girl looked back up at him. "He had me believing that he loved me. But he was no better than the rest." She resisted more tears. "Who are you? Why am I telling you all of this?" The man gave her a gentle smile. "My dear, I'm Judgment. Destiny has chosen you this night to change the course of your life." "Look, mister, if I don't bring enough money back to Raoul, he's gonna change the course of my life by ending it." "Then I will grant you the power of judgment over Raoul." The sadness on the girls face twisted to anger. "Mister, if that were true then I'd make that asshole pay in so many different ways. Sometimes I want to rip his throat out and chop him to pieces. If I had that power, I'd get my revenge." "Perhaps." Judgment turned his head to the right and looked at the night sky. "Perhaps not." He turned his head to the left. Looking directly at the girl, he reached out and grabbed her right hand. The world through her eyes changed from the dark streets to a time past, where a young boy of the age of ten was on the porch of a rundown house, peering through a window. The girl walked up behind the boy to see what he was watching. It was a woman sitting in a chair, giving oral sex to a man. When the man finished, he handed the woman some money. The man was replaced by another, and the woman continued her sordid act. The girl sensed that this boy was Raoul, and the woman was his mother. The scene changed inside the house. Raoul was now inside and the girl watched the mother suffer physical violence. Situation after situation, with many different men—more than she cared to count. Raoul's mother suffered at the hands of the men she brought into her life, and Raoul learned from them disrespect for women. Judgment let go of her hand. "Raoul may be a perpetrator of vile acts, but he too is a victim of abuse," Judgment said. She shook her head. "I didn't know. I never thought of it that way." "The time of judgment is at hand. What is the fate that you choose for Raoul?"

Her eyes were weary now. "Raoul is just a sad man caught up in a crappy environment, just like me. Who knows what he'd be like if his life had been normal? I don't like what he's become, and what he does to me, but I can't hurt him." She sighed. "If only we could break out of the cage we've grown into." "So as you judge, so it will be." Judgment tipped his hat, turned, and walked away. A fat brown envelope lay on the sidewalk where Judgment had been standing. The girl bent cautiously forward and picked it up. Inside was a stack of crisp, one hundred dollar bills, all right side up, and facing the same direction. She counted ten thousand dollars. Destiny had certainly changed her life. Raoul awoke in a large cold room, hanging by his arms from chains connected to the ceiling. The room smelled of vomit, feces, and putrid meat. He swallowed to keep the bile down as it rose up in the back of his throat. His last thoughts before waking up here were of talking to a strange man; someone he wouldn't normally become engaged in a conversation with. He couldn't help himself though, the man had approached him and Raoul was compelled to answer his questions. Raoul's toes just barely touched the floor, and his arms were becoming numb from the blood struggling to flow its way up. He twisted himself around and looked around the room. A chair and a mirror was to one side, and a table with industrial tools and what looked like surgical instruments were to his right, a rusty looking door behind him. The concrete floors were stained in black and auburn, and felt greasy under his feet. The door behind him creaked open, and he spun around in hopes of salvation. It was the well dressed man, the last person he'd talked to. His immediate reaction was to curse and demand to be released, but something about the presence of the man made him hesitate. It wasn't fear, it was uncertainty. The man emanated a power that Raoul felt he wasn't worthy to challenge. He hung in silence, and waited for the man to make his move. Judgment made his way from behind Raoul, placed a bottle of water on the table next to a claw hammer, and stood before his victim. He lit a fresh cigarette. He took a deep draw as the match lit the end, and blew out a stream of smoke towards Raoul. "You may speak," he said. The grip of reverence loosened enough for Raoul to find his voice. "Let me down from here, man, please." Judgment lifted his eyebrows. "I'm sorry, I can't do that. You're here by your own decision." Raoul heard the words, but they made no sense. He hadn't asked to come here, yet there was a connection to the conversation with the man and the reason why he was here. What was it that happened before he blacked out? He remembered he and Judgment were talking—talking about problems, business problems. A territorial dispute between him and a Russian rival that was edging into his business district. Judgment had taken hold of Raoul's hand and his mind was transported back to the past, where he viewed the Russian's life growing up.

When his mind returned to the present, Judgment had asked him to make a choice. Raoul's face lit up when he remembered. "Wait. You got it wrong, man. I said I wanted to make that Ruskie son-of-a-bitch suffer and die. He's messed things up for me big time. What is all of this, why am I here? I ain't done nothin' to deserve this shit." Judgment searched the implements on the table and chose a pair of tweezers and surgical scissors. "I've already told you why you're here." He reached out with the tweezers and pulled Raoul's right eyelid forward, snipping it off with the scissors. Through the cries of his victim's protests, he repeated the action on the left side. "There, now you won't be able to miss any of the excitement," Judgment said. "You're crazy, man, don't do this, please!" Raoul screamed in agony. His bowels quivered and cold fear was now making his entire body numb. Why was this man doing this? What reason did Raoul give to allow this? He couldn't remember. "Why, man, just tell me why?" "So as you judge, so shall you be judged." Judgment selected a stainless steel surgical knife from the table, and started working on his next creation.

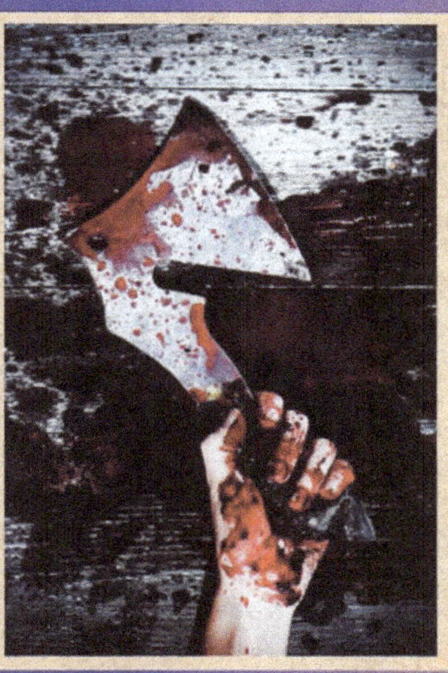
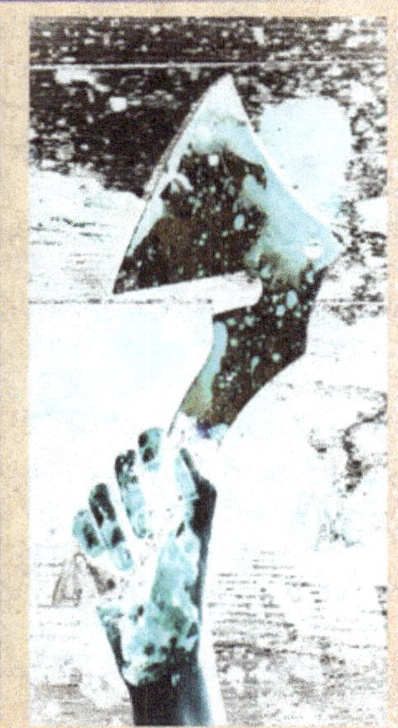

BIKER HEAVEN BY DAVID H. DONAGHE

The year is 1968. LBJ was president and the world was in turmoil. War raged in Southeast Asia, civil unrest raged in the streets of America, and the entire planet seemed to be holding its breath. When the one-two punch came, the world went down for the count and the dead rose from their graves. I was three years back from Vietnam, but all I cared about was drinking, hanging with my bros, and riding my motorcycle. My name is John Brown, but my bros call me Cave Man. I grew up in the biker culture with my dad being one of the founding members of the Road Dogs, a local bike club here in Harlem Springs, Arizona that started in the early fifties. My pops bought me my first bike, a Triumph Bonneville 650, when I was sixteen, but I scrimped, saved, and a year later I bought an old Pan Head. When I turned eighteen, I prospected into the club and I haven't looked back since. Oh, I took a short detour to Vietnam in 1965 to do my patriotic bit, but when I came home, old Bud Hodgkin offered me my job back at the GlenCo station and I fell back into the lifestyle, riding with the club and hanging with my bros. I had just finished putting a new set of tires on Mr. Peterson's Dodge and was sitting in the office, eating my lunch, when the newscast came on the radio. "We interrupt this broadcast for a special news bulletin. We're getting reports from a small town in Iowa, and as strange as it may seem, they're saying that the dead are rising from their graves and attacking the local residents. They appear to have a lust for human flesh, as unbelievable as that sounds. Several people are dead, but amazing as it sounds, after they died, they rose up and joined the ranks of the undead. There are reports of survivors hiding in a farmhouse on the outskirts of town. There are reports of similar incidents occurring across the county. One unconfirmed report states that a Venus probe falling back into Earth's atmosphere may have brought back some type of radiation from outer space. The authorities caution not to panic. They're stressing that people should stay in their homes. The military and police are on high alert and will respond to any outbreak as soon as it's reported." "Zombies. Yeah, right." A chill shot through me when I remembered the graveyard across the street. Then the front window to the office shattered, showering me with shards of broken glass. Looking up, I stared into the cold, dead eyes of a walking corpse. Reaching into the bottom desk drawer, where I kept my Smith and Wesson 357 Magnum, and with my heart beating the shit out of my ribcage, I almost dropped a load in my pants when I realized the gun wasn't there. I'd left my piece in my locker in the back. I jumped to my feet. Looking past the flesh-eating zombie trying to come through the window, I saw more of them coming out of the graveyard in droves. Their wild, feral growls echoed down the street and they slowly dispersed, heading toward different parts of the town.

A large group crossed the road and milled about in the station's parking lot. I stepped into the mechanic's bay only to find it filled with slow-moving zombies. They moved toward me with their arms raised, looking like shit warmed over. Several had maggots crawling underneath their skin and the smell was almost enough to gag a skunk. They had my way blocked both to the roll up door to the outside and to the back room at the rear of the station, where my locker was. Slamming my fist into the face of the nearest zombie, I charged through the undead crowd to a workbench, and grabbed a tire iron. Pulling a knife, I slashed the knife and swung the tire iron, fighting my way toward the back room. Stabbing one zombie in the eye with my knife, I pulled the eye out of its socket with the tip of my blade, and drove the tire iron into the skull of another. Blood splattered over my clothes and I let out a few curses, fighting my way toward the back of the station. I had just reached the door to the back room when one of the bastards bit me on my right arm. Searing hot pain shot through me, making me feel like I was on fire. I let out a scream, drove my blade though the undead thing's face, and watched it fall to the bay floor. Fumbling with my keys, I dropped more of them and let out another curse. After scooping up my keys, I unlocked the door, ran into the back room while feeling the sharp nails of a zombie on my back, and slammed the door and locked it. With shaky hands, I unlocked my locker, grabbed my 357, tucked it into the waistband of my jeans, and grabbed the bottle of Jack Daniels I kept sitting on the top shelf. Taking a pull of whiskey, I let out a sputter and poured half the bottle onto the zombie bite. "Damn that hurts!" I hissed. Looking down at my arm, I noticed that the zombie had bitten me on my arm where my tattoo of a skeletal biker on a chopper was. The bite took a chunk of meat away, taking off the biker's skull. Blood flowed from my wound to drip on the floor, where it pooled at my feet. Taking off my outer shirt, I wrapped it around my bloody arm, binding it up as best I could. "Oh God! Oh shit! I'm fucked!" I yelled. Then the thought hit me, I'm trapped in here. But then I remembered the back window. After stacking some boxes of auto parts, I climbed onto them, broke the back window, and looked out into the alley behind the station. The alley looked clear, so I climbed out the window, jumped to the ground, and ran to the front of the station. Zombies filled the area around the gas pumps, but they were slow movers and I made it to the Pan Head before they noticed me. After climbing on the bike, I came down hard on the kick-starter, but the engine wouldn't start. "Son of a bitch!" I yelled. I gave the kicker another try, and the old Harley rumbled to life. I put it in gear and goosed the throttle, heading straight through the pack of hungry flesh-eaters. Pulling my 357, I popped a cap through the brainpans of two of them, pistol whipped another, and ran over another one before I broke free. Rolling down Main Street, I dodged groups of the undead trying to feed on the town's population.

I noticed a woman sprawled on the ground. An ugly looking zombie in a tattered black suit knelt over her body, pulling intestines from her belly.

Blood and gore covered the street and her dying screams echoed off the surrounding buildings. Another zombie, this one a little girl, shuffled down the street while snacking on a freshly severed human arm. When I passed the town's roller rink, I saw a mob of teenagers come running outside. Several of them had zombie bites and were covered in blood, and they were trying to escape a mop of decaying flesh-eaters lumbering along behind them. Noticing a blonde-headed young girl in a cheerleader's uniform from the neighborhood, I hit the brakes and pulled over to the sidewalk, smoking my tires. "Johnny! Help me!" she screamed. "Hurry up! Climb on!" I yelled. The girl sprinted across the road, jumped onto the back, threw her arms around me, and I gunned the throttle, leaving a patch of rubber on the pavement. "Oh God! It's terrible! Those things are killing everyone!" she screamed. My arm felt like liquid fire. The skin around the bite was starting to rot and seep pus and I felt as if I had hot coals in my belly. Swerving past a gaggle of the undead, we roared down Main Street, turned on Birch and took a quick turn onto Honeysuckle Court. Sliding to a stop in front of my small, run down two-bedroom home, I killed the motor and set the bike on its side stand. "Check on your folks. If you need me yell," I said while climbing off the bike. She darted across the street, ran across her front lawn, and went inside her family home. My portly next door neighbor backed a 1958 Chevy station wagon out of his driveway and slammed on his brakes, giving me a wild, terrified look. "Those things! They attacked my wife and kids. We were sitting down to dinner, but I was in the bathroom when they broke through the back door. There was nothing I could do!" "You might have tried fighting off the sons-of-bitches. Don't you have a gun in the house or a baseball bat?" "Norman! Please help! They're killing us!" his wife screamed from the front door of the house. She let out a blood-curdling scream, but then the screaming stopped as she was pulled back inside. "It's too late. Once they bite you, you're a goner. I'm leaving town," he said. You spineless bastard, I thought and ran into my own house. Inside, I poured some Jack Daniels on my wound, redressed it, then drank the rest of the bottle. Grabbing my jacket, another bottle of Jack, and three boxes of ammo, I ran back outside. Sliding to a stop, I bent over and threw up about half a quart of blood. I noticed small pieces of flesh mixed in with the blood, and the stench was enough to make me throw up again. Cynthia—a girl from across the street—ran over and took my arm. "Are you okay?" "I'm just dandy," I said.

Opening another bottle of Jack, I took a pull from the bottle, letting the numbing whiskey sooth my stomach. "How are things at your house?" "I don't know for sure. There was blood everywhere. I think my parents turned into one of those things." "Let's go," I said. "Where will we go?" "We'll head to the clubhouse. Sonny must have put the word out. We'll probably head to the cabin or fort up at the clubhouse. We've got enough guns and ammo there to fight off an army of these suckers, plus there's food and water." She stopped putting her hands on her pretty little hips. "You've been bitten. You'll turn into one of those things," she said when she saw my arm. "Yeah, maybe, but I'm okay for now. Here," I said, handing her my K-Bar knife. "If I get squirrelly, stab me in the eye or ear. Shove it in hard enough to penetrate the brain." A roar came from the house next door and five of the walking dead lumbered onto the front lawn. Bits and pieces of decayed flesh fell from their skin, and maggots crawled out of their eyes, but the smell; the smell was the enough to make a buzzard puke. "Let's go! Run!" I yelled, sprinting to the bike. Getting onto the saddle, I jumped into the air and came down on the kick-starter. The Pan Head came to life on the third kick, Cynthia climbed onto the back and I goosed the throttle, roaring down the street. I turned onto Main Street, and headed west, weaving through a pack of bloody flesh-eating zombies. Noticing a female zombie on the sidewalk, bent over and ripping the guts out of a small child, I pulled my 357 out with my left hand and put a round through what was left of her brain. At the end of the street, I turned left onto a two-lane highway and increased speed, but so far, the zombies hadn't made it out to the highway. Five miles outside of town, I pulled into the gravel parking lot of the High Noon Saloon. The High Noon, the unofficial clubhouse of the Road Dogs Motorcycle Club, was a rustic-looking bar owned by our club president. Scores of motorcycles and other vehicles filled the parking lot. People carried supplies back and forth from the vehicles to the clubhouse. I parked and Cynthia and I climbed off the bike and headed toward the bar. My stomach felt sick, my legs seemed disjoined, and I felt lightheaded. Noticing my discomfort, Cynthia put her arm around me and helped me into the bar. Several of my bros stood inside, wearing their club vests. Along with what was left of their families, there were a few friends of the club. All eyes turned to me, tracking my movements across the bar to the backroom, where we held our meetings. Our club president, James Taylor, or Sonny as we called him, stood at the bar drinking a rum and coke, talking to our VP, Big Dog. Stumbling up to the bar, I showed Sonny my arm. "I got bit," I said. He let out a low whistle. "That sucks, Cave Man. We've got three others in the same shape." "You know they'll turn into one of those things. We can't take the chance. We've got to leave them here or take them out," Big Dog said. "They're our brothers. We can't just shoot them down," Sonny replied. Laying the pistol down on the bar, I spread my arms apart and put my head down. "Do me if you have to, bro. I'd rather have one of my brothers put one through my brain than turn into one of those things." "Put your gun away. If it comes to that, we'll do what we have to," Sonny said.

Tucking my gun into the waistband of my pants, I looked at the prospect behind the bar. "Give me a Jack and Coke." The prospect fetched my drink and I glanced at Sonny. "Are we heading out to your cabin?" Sonny shrugged. "It's about the safest place, I'd say." "I have a suggestion. I'm dead already. You said the zombies bit three other guys. Let us ride in front. If we run into any of that undead trash, we'll deal with them while you get everyone else to safety." "That sounds like a plan, bro." "So when do we leave?" "As soon as we get packed," Sonny said. "It's starting to get dark now. We'll have to camp in the woods tonight. We need to leave before those things find us." As if on cue, I heard someone scream and a snarl came from out front. "They found us!" someone yelled and then I heard the sound of automatic weapons' fire. Sonny turned and ran to the storeroom with me shuffling along behind him. He tossed me an AR-15. I hobbled toward the front of the bar, broke the front window, and we gazed out at the flesh-eating zombies in the parking lot. Shoulder to shoulder, Sonny and I opened up on the undead fiends with automatic weapons. The zombies banged into each other and fell to the ground under our deadly fire. When the last one fell, Sonny looked at me and said, "Okay, let's get packed." After packing what gear I had onto my bike, I headed to the bathroom and pissed out what looked like syrupy blood. The stench made me puke. Coagulated blood, and chunks of red meat that stunk of decay and stomach bile gushed out of me. Glancing in the mirror, terror shot through me when I realized I didn't look much better than those undead bastards we'd been shooting in the parking lot. My skin had turned pale, legions had formed on my face and small pieces of skin were starting to flake off. The virus was starting to take control and I already felt like one of the undead. A hunger consumed me. When I stepped out of the bathroom, I saw Cynthia and a powerful craving hit me. Visions of me ripping her throat out with my teeth filled my mind. She came up to me and I could see by the look in her face that I scared her. "We're about ready to leave. You ride in one of the cars," I told her. "I'd rather ride with you." "It's not safe. Me and the other guys the zombies bit are gonna lead the caravan and deal with any of them that get in our way. What ever happens, stick with the club. They'll keep you safe." Walking to the front door, Cynthia held on to me, and kept me from falling. I felt like cold shit on a hot bun, but I figured that once I made it to my bike, I'd be all right. We pulled out of the lot heading west on the highway, with us four soon-to- be-dead men leading the caravan. Blood dripped from the corner of my mouth, cold chills racked my body, my vision faded in and out, and my arms felt numb, but I kept my hand on the throttle and rolled down the highway. Ten miles outside of town, we pulled up to a country store at a crossroads. Undead flesh-eaters milled about in the parking lot and blocked the road. I saw a female zombie ripping the throat out of a poor, elderly woman lying on the ground near the gas pumps. The zombie wore no shirt and her putrid decaying flesh sagged down.

Me and the other three bikers gunned our throttles, plowed into the horde blocking the road, and tried to clear a path. We hit the brakes, coming to a stop, and had a rumble with the undead. Pulling my 357, I sat on my bike with my pistol in one hand and my knife in the other. All four of us sat on our bikes, slashing and shooting while the rest of the convoy escaped. Every time one of the undead things got too close, I would kick it away with my feet and either stab or shoot it. The sound of their wild growling along with the gunshots and a few shouted curse words echoed down the highway. "Let's go!" I yelled, once the convoy had made it clear of the undead mob. Doing a burn out, I rolled over a zombie wearing a tattered cowboy hat and gunned the throttle. Sweat dripped from my pores, running like a river down my side. Chills racked my body and I felt feverish, but I managed to keep the bike under control. Spitting out a mouthful of blood and a chunk of my stomach lining, I pulled a bottle of Jack from the pocket of my club vest. Chugging the potent brew, I wondered how long I had until death came knocking and turned me into one of those things. Weaving back and forth, I looked into my rearview mirror and almost fell out off the seat. I looked like a three-day-old corpse on a motorcycle. My cheeks had turned hollow, and had lost all their color, and I noticed more pieces of dead flesh flaking off. Glancing down at my arm, I saw open sores, which exposed the bone beneath, and the stench was enough to make a maggot shit. I thought about my brothers up ahead in the convoy and wondered, What if I turn? I don't want to hurt one of my bros. Glancing over at my three dead brothers riding along with me, I was shocked to see that they looked worse than me. They looked exactly like what they were: dead men on motorcycles, but they just didn't know it yet. I remembered that verse in the Bible about the four horsemen of the apocalypse. The sun had barely gone down when my brother Chops—a short stocky man with pork chop sideburns—started losing control of his bike. His head dropped to his chest and then snapped up violently. A wild crazy look crossed his face, foam came from his mouth, and he let out a tortured growl. His bike went sideways and then swerved and fell over, launching him onto the pavement. I swerved to the right, the two other remaining zombie bikers swerving left, as a pack of motorcycles swarmed around him and the first four-wheeled vehicle in the convoy rolled over him. The bike slid to the edge of the road. Chops stood up and lumbered off into the forest, now very dead, and dragging his broken body along with him. After the convoy passed, I whirled the Pan Head around and rode back to where Chops disappeared into the forest. Parking along side of the road, I pulled my 357 and peered out into the woods. I could hear him growling. He turned around, coming out of the forest, and he approached me with his arms outstretched. He had a hungry, feral look in his eyes that I sympathized with, because the lust for human flesh filled my innermost being as well. Visions of torn throats and butchered bodies filled my head. Chops let out a hungry cry. He struggled up an embankment with his arms stretched out, ready to bite and tear with his teeth.

"I'm sorry, bro. I can't leave you like this," I said and shot him in the forehead with my 357. The sound of the gunshot echoed through the trees, and his body tumbled down the embankment, dead for good this time. Leaning over, I puked up blood mixed with bits of meat. I climbed back on my bike and kicked it over, then spun the bike around and headed down the highway. Pulling my bottle of Jack from my coat pocket, I downed half the bottle in one shot. The bike weaved back and forth, but I didn't know if it was because of my weakened condition, or the fact that I was drunk. We rolled on through the night, passing through a pine forest without seeing anymore of the undead, and I could barely stay awake. My head throbbed, my arms felt numb, my vision turned fuzzy, my belly felt as if it were on fire, and to top if off, I ran out of liquor. Around midnight, Sonny flashed his lights, and the convoy pulled off the road and into a small clearing. The drivers of the four-wheeled vehicles formed a circle with their headlights facing inward and the bros pulled their bikes into the center of the circle. It reminded me of the pioneer days when they circled the wagons. I parked my bike, put down the kickstand, and fell to the ground. Struggling to my feet, I puked up blood and tried to ignore the hunger burning inside me. Images of me ripping the flesh off my brothers flashed through my head yet again. Feeling my stomach churn, I ran into the forest, pulled down my pants and let go with a gush that was more blood than shit. Ignoring the stench, I wiped with leaves, pulled up my pants, and stumbled back into the clearing. The other two zombie bikers looked in no better shape than me. Sonny sauntered up to us. "Hey, bro. You look like shit." "I feel like shit," I said. "I feel like ten pounds of dog shit in a five pound bag." "We should reach the cabin before noon tomorrow. Do you think you can hold on that long?" "You saw what happened to Chops. We don't have much time left." "Is there anything I can do for you, bro? I hate seeing you like this." "Tie us up to one of these trees," I said, motioning to the other zombie bikers. "If we die during the night, we won't be able to hurt anyone." "We'll do that. I'm sorry, bro. I wish there was more we could do for you." "Get me another bottle of Jack, and Sonny, If I turn into one of those things, put me down like a rabid dog," I said, seeing the reflection of tears in Sonny's eyes. "You know I will, bro. I won't leave you like that," he said, his voice cracking slightly. After they tied each of us around the waist to three stout trees outside the camp, I poured some Jack Daniels onto my zombie bite, flinched from the sting, and let out a curse. My brother, leaning against the tree next to me, noticed my 357 tucked into the waistband of my jeans. "Hey, man, if I die during the night and turn into one of those things, splatter my brains with that hog leg." "Sure thing, Old School. I'll set the piece between us. If I turn, you to do the same to me." "Don't forget about me, Cave Man. I don't feel so good. I don't think I got much time left," the brother sitting next to Old School said. "Sure thing, Teddy Bear. I'll do the right thing," I replied.

A few minutes later, Cynthia knelt down next to me with the pale moonlight reflecting off her pretty face. "Oh Johnny. I'm so sorry for what happened. Thank you for taking me with you." I gazed at the tender flesh of her neck, the soft curve of her breasts, and felt the hunger. "Cynthia, you need to back away from me. The virus is changing me. Believe me, baby, when I say this, I'm not being a dirty old man. I feel like eating you up. I mean it in the most literal sense. I feel a hunger in me that I can't satisfy." "You could never hurt me," she whispered. "No, listen to me, baby. When we get to the cabin, you'll be safe. After a while things will calm down. When things are normal, find yourself a nice young dude and settle down. Live your life and maybe every now and then, toss back a beer for old Cave Man." She leaned forward, ignoring the stench of my decaying flesh, and kissed me. "I'm so sorry, Johnny," she whispered as warm tears rolled down her cheeks. Taking a pull from the bottle of Jack, I ignored the hunger, and watched her run back to camp. It seemed like I had just dropped off when a wild snarl and people yelling woke my from a vicious nightmare involving the ripping and tearing of flesh. To my right, Teddy Bear struggled against the ropes binding him to the tree. He snapped with his teeth, clawed with his hands, as he tried to get at Old School and me. Frothy foam and blood dripped from his mouth. Sometime during the night, his body gave up the fight and he joined the ranks of the undead. Old School leaned away from him, trying to keep from getting bit. "Shoot him, man! Shoot him!" Old School yelled. Grabbing the 357, I leaned across Old School's lap and stuck the barrel against the side of Teddy Bear's head. "I'm sorry, bro," I said and pulled the trigger, splattering Teddy Bear's brains onto the forest floor. Sonny and several other bros came running up. Sonny knelt down next to me and I saw tears in his eyes. "He's in a better place now, bro. You need to get some brothers and bury him," I said. "We'll take care of it, brother. You two just hold on," Sonny said. He leaned forward, ignoring the stench, and gave us both a quick hug. Old School and I sat tied to the tree and watched them drag Teddy Bear's remains away for burial. "I don't want to go out like that, man," Old School said after the excitement was over. "I don't either, bro. I'd rather go out like a biker, on the road. We've got to hang in there until we reach the cabin. Then you and me will head out on our own. We'll let the road take us." We sat passing the bottle of Jack back and forth for about a half hour and then drifted off into a pitiful, tortured sleep. The sound of doors slamming woke me a few hours later from another violent nightmare. Chills shook my body, my head felt hot, clammy sweat rolled down the side of my face, my vision was fuzzy, and my stomach lurched. Warm fingers of sunlight stabbed across the land and the smell of cooking food drifted on the wind. Sonny brought Old School and me a plate loaded with scrambled eggs, bacon and fried potatoes. "I don't know if I can eat that, bro," I said. "You need to keep your strength up," Sonny told me. "Why? You know we ain't getting' any better." "I know, bro. We're pulling out of here in an hour or so. We should make it to the cabin by noon. I'm hoping you guys will make it that far at least."

"We'll try, bro, but promise me something. If we turn before we get there, put us down quick." "You know I will," Sonny said. I ate my breakfast and promptly threw it up. A stinky mixture of blood, stomach bile, and undigested eggs shot out of me and covered the ground. Old School only took a couple of bites of his food, but he didn't have any better luck keeping it down than I did. We broke camp at eight that morning and Old School and I were set free. I noticed our bros giving us sideways glances, while keeping their hands close to the handguns riding on their hips. Old School and I lumbered over to our motorcycles, stumbling along on legs that didn't want to move right. The hunger burned inside of us like a raging inferno, and Old School noticed one of our old ladies climbing into a station wagon. "You know, she's got a nice ass, but right now I'd rather rip off her arms and gnaw on her bones," Old School said. "I know, man. It's the disease. When Cynthia came over to talk with me last night, it was all I could do to keep from ripping her throat out. We've just got to hang in there until we reach the cabin." We climbed on our motorcycles, barely able to stand up, and rumbled down the highway. I glanced in my left rearview mirror, and my eyes widened and my jaw dropped. My face looked skeletal, my flesh had turned purple, puss oozed from legions on my cheeks, and I noticed a maggot crawl out of one of the sores. Skin flaked off my face, exposing the meat beneath. God, no wonder my bros were looking at me weird, I thought. Old School and I weaved back and forth, trying to maintain control. Four hours later, we pulled off the highway onto the dirt road leading to the cabin. Before turning off the highway, a large oak tree next to the road, a hundred yards west of the turn off, caught my eye. The road headed through the trees, passing through a dense forest and then snaked its way uphill. At the top of the hill, the road descended into a small punch bowl shaped valley. The cabin was in the center of the valley in the middle of a grassy meadow. An old barn and a couple of outbuildings were off to the left. Behind the cabin, a stream meandered across the valley. The convoy pulled up to the cabin and parked, and everyone began to unload equipment. Sonny assigned work details and stationed people with guns at various points to act as security. Old School and I walked over to the barn, trying to get away from the bright sunlight. "Did you see that oak tree down the road near the turn off?" I asked Old School. "Yeah," he said. He bent over, throwing up blood. "If we hit that tree at about a hundred miles an hour without a helmet, it should splatter our heads like a couple of ripe melons." "That should do it. We'd best get it done while we still have time," he agreed. Sonny entered the barn. "How're you guys feeling?" "Like shit warmed over," I said. "We're gonna pull out of here. Our plan is to let the road take us and die like bikers should. We don't want to turn into one of those zombie sons-of-bitches." Sonny had tears in his eyes when he spoke, and his voice cracked. "Okay, I'll gather the crew. We'll send you off right."

Fifteen minutes later, the sound of Harleys rumbled through the forest as we prepared to head back to the highway. Cynthia came running out when we were about to leave and insisted on coming with us. She jumped onto the back of my bike and wrapped her arms around me. The Road Dogs lined up on the road. Old School and I parked our bikes in front of the pack facing west and then climbed off our motorcycles to say good-bye. Cynthia clung to my arm with tears running down her face. Even though we smelled like five day old road kill, and our skin oozed puss, our brothers grabbed each of us in bear hugs and we did some back slapping. "I wish there was something we could do for you, bro," Sonny said, wiping tears from his eyes. "It's cool, man. Listen, sometime hold a party for Old School and me, huh? Toast us and say our names." "You can count on it, bro," Sonny said, handing me a bottle of Jack Daniels. I downed half the bottle, handed it to Old School, and he gulped down the rest. Cynthia hugged me and then kissed me on my decaying cheek. "Thank you for taking me with you, Johnny, I can never repay you." "You go find yourself a good decent young man and live a good life. That's how you can repay me." "I'll never forget you, Johnny," she whispered and stepped back. Sonny put his arm around her, trying to comfort her. I looked at Old School and nodded my head. "Let's ride, bro," I said and then stumbled onto my Harley. Old School staggered to his bike and we climbed into the saddle. Behind us, our brothers fired up their engines and revved their throttles, giving us a royal send off. I came down on the kick-starter of my bike, firing up the old Pan Head and Old School fired up his Knuckle Head. He pulled his bike up next to mine and stopped. "Let's do this," I said, glancing down the road. I engaged the transmission, released the clutch, and cranked the throttle. The back tire spun, and I shot down the road. I kept my fist on the throttle. Glancing in my mirror, I saw Old School on my tail. The needle on the speedometer climbed up to fifty while I shifted through the gears, and once I hit fifth gear, I cranked the throttle wide open. The needle shot up to one hundred and ten miles an hour and I swerved to the side of the road, heading straight for the large oak tree. In my rearview, I saw Old School still on my tail. Things happened in a matter of milliseconds. I slammed into the tree with a violent jolt, and the impact launched me over the handle bars. Old School plowed into the back of my bike and I caught a flash of his body catapulting over me. The last thing I saw and felt was my head hitting the tree, then the world went white. I didn't know how much time had passed but I found myself whole and feeling fine. The virus running through me was gone. Old School and I stood up and stepped out onto the side of the road. "I guess it didn't work. I guess we turned into one of them zombies anyway," I said. "I don't think so, bro. Look," Old School said, turning around and pointing to the shoulder of the road. I saw our mangled bodies among the wreckage of our bikes. Both of our heads looked like smashed watermelons. Glancing up the road, I saw our club brothers coming our way. "I don't think they can see us," I said. "What are we? Ghosts?" "I don't feel like a ghost, and we don't look like ghosts either.

Look at your arm where you got bit," Old School said. I held up my arm and my eyes widened with joy. My skin looked healthy, the zombie bite was gone. The pack rumbled down to the crash site and Sonny climbed off his bike. "Little Mike, go back and get one of the pickup trucks. We'll take them back and bury them behind the cabin. Have one of the guys bring another truck to take what's left of their rides back," Sonny said. "What do we do now?" Old School asked. We stood watching our brothers pick up our bodies and load up our mangled motorcycles. "I don't know, but it's a shame we had to wreck our bikes like that. I hope they can fix 'em." "I know what you mean, bro. I hate to see a good ride go down." The sound of loud pipes reverberated through the surrounding forest, but the members of the Road Dogs loading up the motorcycles and the bodies didn't seem to notice. "Hey, Cave Man, check this out. Someone's coming," Old School said. I glanced up the road and saw five motorcycles heading our way, but they were like no other bikes I'd ever seen. They seemed to radiate light. Their colors looked more vivid than anything I'd ever seen, and their chrome seemed brighter than the sun. They rumbled up next to us and came to a stop. "Hey, I know these guys," I said to Old School. "There's Hondo. He died on I-40 three years ago. There's Little Danny Boy. He bought it in Vietnam. And that's Hector and Iron Man; they bought the farm that time when that outlaw club jumped us. That other guy's Thumper. He crashed into a car last year." Little Danny Boy, a wiry little man with a scraggly goatee, walked over and caught me up in a big bear hug. "What are you guys doing here?" I asked. "We're here to take you home, man. Check out your new rides." I looked onto the road and my mouth fell open. There were two of the most beautiful looking motorcycles I'd ever seen. They hadn't been there before and I knew right away which one was mine. It looked like my dream bike, only ten times better than I could ever imagine. The colors looked more radiant than anything I'd ever seen and the chrome, well, I could hardly look at the chrome, it was so bright. "What's this?" I asked, still not believing it. "Those are your spirit bikes, bro." Noticing a shimmering light down the road, where the road climbed a steep hill, I saw what looked like an emerald city that reminded me of Cibola, the legendary city of gold that the Spanish Conquistadors came searching for back in the day. "What's that place up there?" I asked. "That's Biker Heaven, man. That's where we're going," Little Danny Boy said. "It's not all angels and harps, is it?" Old School asked. "Hell no, bro. I said we're going to Biker Heaven. It's a constant party where the brew flows freely and the women are loose." "Will I still get to ride my bike?" I asked. "Hell yeah, man. You haven't ridden until you've ridden one of these babies. What's cool is that you don't have to put gas in 'em and they don't leak oil. And we can ride for eternity if we want to." I shook my head in disbelief. "You know, Danny Boy, I've lived a wild life. I always thought I was going to the other place."

Old School stepped up, listening to our conversation with a big grin on his face. Little Danny Boy smiled. "Do you remember back in the 'Nam when you risked your life to save me?" "Yeah, but you still died." "Yeah, I died, but you saved five other guys and got yourself shot." "I was just doing my duty, trying to save my bros." "How about that time you tried to save Hector and Iron Man from that outlaw club? You stood over them, fighting like a wild man until help arrived." I shrugged. "Yeah, but again, they still died." "But you tried, man. That's what counts. You were willing to lay down your life for your bros. What about that girl—Cynthia? If you hadn't stopped to help her, she'd be one of them undead things right now. And you stayed with the club and saw our brothers to safety, even though you wanted to rip their throats out." "Yeah, but anyone of those guys would have done the same for me." "Maybe. But the Good Book says that 'greater love has no man then when he lays down his life for his friends.' You were willing to do that on numerous occasions in your lifetime. You're famous in Biker Heaven, man. We're gonna throw you a welcome party like you've never seen. Get on your ride, bro. We're headin' home." "What about booze? Can we drink up there?" I asked. "Hell yeah, man! You can drink all you want and you don't get a hangover in the morning," Little Danny Boy said and tossed me a bottle of Jack. I cracked open the bottle, took a swallow, and enjoyed the feel of liquid fire running down into my belly. It tasted better than anything I'd ever had. I handed Old School the bottle, and he took a long pull and grinned. "Let's go home, bro," I said to Old School who nodded in reply. We walked out to the road and climbed onto our new motorcycles. Little Danny Boy took up his position in front as Road Captain, and the pack formed up behind him. Old School and I fell in at the rear. Goosing the throttle, I headed down the highway and put my face in the wind.

LDP: What type of mediums do you work with?

GM: These days it's almost all digital work. Photoshop mostly, although I've been dabbling in Painter lately. I used to work in pen and ink and I've spent years developing a digital style that mimics ink work. It just saves so much time working digitally, no worries about running out of titanium white at midnight. Or realizing the pen tip you just broke is your last one and having to lose half a day going to get more. Besides the fact that prices for 'regular' art supplies are going through the roof - when you can even find them. I used to use a certain brush for my ink work, when I last checked, they were over twenty dollars. Doing a comic story, I might go through five or more of them.

LDP: What inspired you to be an artist?

GM: It's something I've been interested in for as long as I can remember. My mother used to sit me down with paper, crayons, and pencils and I'd draw for hours. It's a really therapeutic feeling. Of course it wasn't always that way. I've broken many illustration boards and torn up countless pages in my time while trying to get the images in my mind to look the same on paper. Not so much lately. I think as we get older, things effect us differently and we look for and enjoy different things. Recently I've realized that what I enjoy is the DOING of the art, not as much what it comes to. Getting to be the second coming of Frazetta isn't going to happen but working on art and challenging myself will (hopefully) always be there.

LDP: Do you feel that people are born with artistic talent, or that it's something that can be learned?

GM: I really don't go for that 'God's given you a gift' thing. I worked for and sweated for and sometimes bled for every line in every piece. You're talking years and years of doing this. Yes, I love it, but that doesn't change that it's a difficult thing to learn. On the other hand, I think that we all might have a 'hint' or a push in a certain direction in life. Probably most of the time something happens to derail that push. But sometimes things fall into place to follow that direction. But again, that's no guarantee of anything. One of my old teachers used to say we've all got a chance to achieve our potential. Hold your hands apart a foot or two. You've got to get from your right hand to your left. Now, at any time you're somewhere between the two hands but you never know where. Maybe an inch for where you want to be, maybe a foot. The problem is to try to keep going as far as you can. You may give up just before you get there or life may throw in an obstacle you can't overcome.

LDP: What do you think is the biggest change from Old-world art to modern day art?

GM: Probably the accessibility of art to almost anyone who wants it. Well, maybe just more accessibility than in the past. With all the budget cuts and foreclosures and layoffs going on, (I better not get started on where I think this country is headed) I think maybe art is going to drop back to being something for the wealthy and the lucky again. I think, still, in a many cases, if someone wants to, they can pursue art.

LDP: What do you think traditional/classic art can teach about horror in history?

GM: Everything. Traditional/classic art should be the beginning of anyone's studying if they want to be an artist of any kind. You can look at the bulk of mainstream comics if you want to see what happens if you only look at the currently popular artist when you're starting your career. I think that holds true for writing too. If you haven't read Frankenstein or Dracula, or even War of the Worlds for that matter, it's doubtful you're going to add much new to the genre. And I wonder how many people these days realize how much the zombie field owes to Richard Matheson's I Am Legend.

LDP: Do you ever use symbolism in your art?

GM: I do but not really to make any kind of statement. More just to amuse myself and try to get deeper into the piece. You probably feel this in writing when you hit a point and the work just takes off - almost on it's own. Trying to make little connections in the work seems to help me get a step away from the actual work and let my subconscious take over.

LDP: Can you think of a popular piece of art that really should be categorized as horror art?

GM: Sure, check out most of Francisco Goya's work. Or Rembrandt's bible paintings.

LDP: Does horror writing help you draw?

GM: Definitely, my reading habits and art choices are totally linked. I've been reading horror and sci-fi for as long as I can remember. My earliest sketchbooks are filled with dinosaurs and giant sharks! I knew I wanted to be an illustrator because I'd always be drawing scenes from the books I read. There's a lot of Edgar Rice Burroughs and Robert E Howard pictures in my old sketchbooks along with spaceships and alien monsters. A good book can be an inspiration. Even a lousy one can have a scene that would be fun to draw.

LDP: How do you feel about professional critique?

GM: I love to get comments on my work. It's really one of the best ways to improve. We can keep pushing ourselves and learning new techniques, but another pair of eyes is always going to see a picture differently. Critiques can sting a little but it only helps make you a better artist. My wife always sees my art before it goes out into the world.

LDP: As an artist, what lured you to dabble in the macabre?

GM: Again, it was influences in my childhood. I have two older brothers who watched a lot of horror and sci-fi movies when we were kids. Saturdays would have Creature Feature, or they'd bring home a Creepy or Eerie magazine. I remember begging my parents to let me stay up late to watch King Kong (remember back then, if you didn't catch a movie when it was on, you might have to wait years to see it again, if ever). And of course I had a nightmare that same night.

LDP: Do you think science fiction has an influence in the horror art genere?

GM: Yeah, I think they're both linked pretty closely. Not many recent sci-fi films haven't had at least some horror in them. 'Sunshine', 'Cloverfield', 'Inception', the Predator and Alien series. With both of those last two you've got something that will track and kill you with very little chance you can fight back. 'Alien' is far above the predator movies, though, in my opinion. The first half hour or so of 'District 9' was fantastic. The tension it built up before it became another run of the mill sci-fi/adventure movie was amazing, edge of your seat storytelling, then they dropped the ball. In the print world, Connie Willis's Doomsday Book has scenes more horrific and unsettling than most recent horror. And Dan Simmons goes to some pretty dark places as well, in his science fiction.

LDP: What is one of your favorite horror films, and has it affected your art?

GM: 'King Kong' just left a huge impression on me as a kid and it's still a great horror movie, 'Alien' though, is one of those stories that take a handful of characters, put them in a closed situation (I mean you can't just run away and go home) and then let them live or die based on their personalities. To me that's the perfect set up for horror. Some film makers pull it off and some don't.

LDP: Do you aim for a specific audience, or do you feel your art may appeal to the general public?

GM: I figure the people who like my stuff are on the same wavelength as I am. I usually find that we share some of the same likes and dislikes. I doubt a lot of my work will appeal to the general public. Maybe things like my Oz and Alice in Wonderland pieces.

LDP: Do you think that digital art is as valid an art form as traditional mediums?

GM: Yeah, that's all I work in for the most part. I don't really see how someone could claim it wasn't valid unless they didn't know anything about how it works. In that case they shouldn't really be making those kinds of statements (not that that stops anyone these days). One of the best compliments I've gotten (whether it was meant as one or not) was when a fellow artist saw one of my old non-digital paintings and said it looked just like my digital stuff. And people have been surprised that my recent black and white line work art isn't pen and ink.

That's the whole point to me - you want the work to look like YOU want it to. regardless of medium. A lot of the current digital work in the mainstream looks too slick to me, like the artist is relying on the programs to decide the look of the piece.

LDP: Animation viewed as art in motion is a great phenomenon; would you like to be an animator? And if so, what kind of animation would you produce?

GM: Back when I started at the Joe Kubert School, we had a choice of going into the illustration department or the animation department. I chose the illustration, because back then, animation seemed like more of a group effort. And it seemed like it would be particularly difficult to develop a particular kind of style or get recognition. But now, with computer animation, it seems that individual artists, or a small group of artists are able to make much more personal films. So yeah, somewhere down the line I would like to learn and do some animation. There are some stories that can only be best told with movement and sound. And also the freedom that created artwork gives over human actors.

LDP: Can you think of an incident of real horror that might have compelled you to produce horror art?

GM: No, not really, I've seen some horrible things but not that effects my art. I don't think of my horror stuff to be related to the real world for the most part. That's why I like doing monsters and zombies etc - a Yeti isn't going to be chasing you through the snow. Even that cannibal piece I did (Book of Cannibals 2: The Hunger) bothered me because it's something that really could happen (far fetched as it seems), and similar things HAVE happened. I'm very happy with the finished piece though! But a zombie attack is still fantasy (for now anyway).

LDP: Like Vampires and Werewolves before them, the Zombie genre is changing in current form, what type of Zombies do you feel are scarier, running ghouls or walking ones?

GM: It depends on the situation. If you've got space to move or not. The running ghouls are scary in that they WANT to kill you but something about the slow shambling ones that want to tear you apart just to eat you with no real malice (they just NEED to) is somehow scarier to me.

LDP: Do you feel there is a credible difference in sensual art and pornographic art?

GM: That's a tough one. It's a personal opinion - I've seen amazing well done art that's porno to me but to someone else the fact that it's well done may take it above that. The problem becomes who's deciding this and who are they deciding it for. It's like a parent deciding they don't want their child reading a particular book so they want it banned for everyone else too.

LDP: Do you think that comics/graphic novels can ever be taken as a serious art form in the mainstream world of art?

GM: I'm not sure why they would want to be. I mean, so much of the mainstream is filled with posers and wanna-a-be posers (also known as mainstream critics). Besides, the mainstream seems to be using comics as their candy box now anyway. 'Lets do THIS as a movie' 'But of course we have to change it because it's not good enough as it is' which translates to not understanding the genre and the differences in medium. Pick almost any comic book movie. It's usually an actor who carries the film - not the story itself.

LDP: Have you ever thought of making a career out of something other than art - if so, then what?

GM: No, I never really have. For better or worse, this is what I've always wanted to do. I can't imagine not wanting to do this or not knowing what I want to do with my time.

LDP: Lastly, where can people view your art, and how can viewers buy some of your work, or contact you?
GM: You can look for me at: http://foggie32.deviantart.com/ or look me up on Facebook.
LDP: Thanks so much Gary, we can't wait to see more of your work in the future.
GM: Not a problem, it was a pleasure.

The Lonely Necromancer by Kevin James Breaux

After eight long years of medical school and two years of working diligently in the field, Norman Mixter was finally ready to focus on a relationship. This was word for word how he started off all his e-dating chats. Norman loathed telling women he never really had a serious girlfriend before, so he blamed his single status on his studies. Nothing deflected their questions like his degree, Dr. Norman Mixter—the ladies loved the sound of it as much as he did. Norman was a stickler for time management. Time, as they said, was a commodity and when you worked in forensics, with dead bodies, you were constantly reminded of how fragile life was. Every human being owned a piece of time, but it could be taken away abruptly, snatched away by the greedy hand of death. Norman knew everyone owned a piece of death, too, but that was a theory he didn't share with his colleagues. While straightening the empty cans of energy drinks that sat cock-eyed on his home office desk, he copied and pasted one of his standard answers from a FAQ spreadsheet he'd created. Tonight's chat was with a woman from the suburbs, a divorcee who liked to consider herself a bit of a cougar. Norman was thirty-three years old, well beyond the age range of cougar bait, but the e-dating servers had matched him with her. As a matter of fact they matched him with a lot of women. Norman may have been a forensic scientist, but he well understood computers and numbers, too. He figured out, months ago, how to answer the initial questions of the e-dating survey in a way that would produce the most matches. He was proud of his work regardless of the wide variety of ladies it produced, even the stud-hungry cougars. He was no pretty boy and he couldn't be called rugged either. If he had to be categorized by his looks, he would have fallen in with the Bill Gates, Al Gore and Donald Trump types. Good looking, to those who found power desirable, but few saw him for even that, as he didn't show his true powers in public. Norman worked nights in of all places, a town that never slept, Las Vegas. Raised in Phoenix and schooled in Los Angles, he was accustomed to the heat and the continuous buzz of excitement, yet he preferred the night. The evening air smelled different and carried in it a charge of energy that made all things seem possible. With that vigor came sin, which often lead to death, and death was Norman's job. Chief Forensic Anthropologist, was his title at the Las Vegas Police Department and it wasn't just a job, as he would say in jest during chats with possible dates, it was a lifestyle he took very serious. Too prideful to see it, he would never understand that his job disturbed women more than impressed them.

The collective sigh of disappointed women he met online wishing his doctorate was that of a surgeon instead, could deafen the most hard of hearing. Tonight's chat with Kelly was going great. She didn't seem bothered by his profession, in fact she was intrigued. The chat window chimed with each question she asked, becoming almost rhythmic with its frequency. Norman smiled from ear to ear, took a sip of his drink, and typed in a new reply. Building the courage to do the unthinkable, he reached down to pet his ridgeback dog, Shelley. "Think I should ask her out to dinner? Or maybe just a quick coffee?" he asked his pooch. Although his dog didn't reply, the answer was obvious. After clicking away at the keys on his laptop, he enthusiastically tapped enter with his index finger, mouthing the word 'engage.' A few seconds passed, long enough for the pressure to produce a bead of sweat on his brow. Then came release in the form of a one word answer. Yes. "With any luck I should be home in about two, maybe three hours," he told his dog as he stood. Forty-five minutes later, Norman reentered his home, head hung low, yet another failed date. "Kelly was probably thirty pounds heavier than her picture, but she said I wasn't what I represented myself as. Can you believe that, Shelley?" She barked and wagged her tail before jumping up to his lap. At least she loved him. Tomorrow would be a better day. Norman knew it. Returning to work, he found that his officemate Steve had finally come back from vacation. Two weeks on some Caribbean Island, but that wasn't why Norman would utter the words, 'lucky bastard.' Gazing down at the new addition to Steve's desk—a framed 5x7 photo of he and his wife Stephanie—Norman's eyes were glued to the most logical focal point, her yellow bikini-clad breasts. Norman had always found Stephanie attractive. In her late twenties, the beach blonde had an amazing set of tits, which, in no matter what picture, were always on full display. Stephanie was what the other married men in the office referred to as a 'trophy wife,' and Norman couldn't agree more. What a prize a woman like she was. Caught staring, Steve slapped him on the shoulder, rousing Norman from his daydream as Steve entered the room. "That was taken on the beautiful, white beaches of Antigua, bud," Steve said proudly. Steve's voice carried a tone of mockery. I bet you wish you were there went unsaid, but for Norman it was the warm wetness of the Caribbean ocean he was jealous of.

"Have you ever seen a happier lady, Norman?" Steve was getting closer to the bulls-eye. "No, never." "No worries, pal, you'll find yours someday." Walking away from the growing tension in the room, Norman placed his bag down on his desk. Not watching how it settled, the bag tipped to the floor where two books and a saran-wrapped sandwich spilled out. "Careful there, buddy." After plucking up the one book, which slid near his feet, Steve read the spine. "Not this one again! How many times have your read Frankenstein?" "Seven or eight times I guess," Norman replied, the second book that had fallen gripped tightly in his hand. "What's that one?" Steve inquired curiously. "Greek and Roman Necromancy, by Ogden." "I take it back," he nodded with distaste. Looking at him, full of honest confusion, Norman asked what he meant by his statement. "You're never gonna find a chick reading that weird crap." "But I…" "Let's get to work," Steve said, closing the discussion abruptly. It was far from a hard day of work, and Norman's tasks were simple. His department had exhumed the body of a murder victim a few days ago and he was the lucky man set to examine the remains. It was a cold case, fifteen years aged at that. Norman remembered reading about the crime when he was in high school. Particularly high profile, due to the prime suspect, a well-respected heart surgeon. The case went on and on until Bradley Cole—the man in question—was found dead. Recent breakthroughs in science added this case to the ones the L.V.P.D wanted to revisit during any 'slowness.' After following a few leads, the court finally followed through with an order to exhume Megan Gate, just nineteen when she was found dead on the side of the road. Very little shocked Norman, but treating the dead like trash always bothered him. Even Neanderthals buried their dead. Norman knew the facts well, having written a few articles on ancient ceremonial burial. Plastic tarps weren't burial shrouds, he would state in his current report. This undertaking was exciting and a refreshing change from the daily grind, but there was one thing, a thorn in the side of this rose-like day. It was that damn picture of Stephanie. Stealing glances at it any chance he could, Norman found his focus split between wanting to discover what hidden secrets were buried with the bones of this victim and the daydream of enjoying sweet warmth between Stephanie's legs. A sting of loneliness pricked his heart, growing with intensity throughout the day, until he felt as if he would have a myocardial infarction. Tomorrow would be a better day, he hoped. Norman got to work early. It was Thursday night and bad things always seemed to happen on Thursday nights. To the residents, it felt like this night was a warm-up for Friday night, when the amateurs really flooded the city and the professional criminals went to work. Half expecting his boss to have a fresh file to hand him when he walked in the door, Norman noticed a distinct feeling of gloom as he walked to his office.

Backtracking, he tried to discover what had happened without being too obvious. Standing at the counter where the coffee machine was, he overheard two of the clerks reveal just that. "So he just found her dead when he came home?" the louder of the two women asked. "He said she was still warm. He's really beating himself up over not heading directly home after work. He thinks maybe she had an allergic reaction or something." "Well, I've seen her pop a few pills at office parties, if you know what I mean." The woman's salacious words peaked Norman's attention. "No!" "Yep!" "Just, anxiety meds right?" "Sure, aren't we all a little stressed?" the boisterous clerk rolled her eyes as she spoke. "How's Steve handling it?" Norman dropped the mug of coffee he'd just filled the instant he heard his officemate's name. Steve, if they were talking about him then they must mean… "Stephanie?" Norman asked, when the two chatting ladies turned their heads in the direction of the shattering mug. "Hey there, Norman," the softer-spoken woman said with a smile. "Yeah, can you believe it? Stephanie's dead!" Norman shuffled at an accelerated pace to his office, shutting the door behind him. His mind was swimming with crazy thoughts, one more bizarre than the other. Swelling with images, desires and fantasies, he couldn't make his brain stop. Digging through his bag, he retrieved a little orange bottle, one filled with pills for just this occasion. He had to resist what was awakening inside him; he may have had the thoughts, but that didn't make him… Creek. Rattle. When the door to his office unexpectedly opened behind him Norman fumbled the bottle, spilling its contents to the floor. "I was just…" Norman began, until he saw it was Steve standing behind him. "Hey, guy, I have an important request for you." Shocked that the man was even at work today, although noting his lack of business attire and puffy, tear-stained eyes, Norman stood with mouth agape, wanting to say something profound but only releasing a scratchy gasp. "My wife," Steve sniffled. "She died last night, I…" "I'm so sorry," Norman finally said. "I don't know how or why?" Steve paused, rubbing both his hands over his face. "You…you know how to do a post-mortem examination, right?" "You mean an autopsy?" Norman asked curiously. "Y…yes, just don't say it that way, okay, man?" "I'm a licensed coroner. Fall back job, you know? Just in case this one…" Norman was giving too much information, something he did when he was faced with such uncomfortable moments. "Good, 'cause I need you to do me a big favor." Steve held his breath and stabilized his words. "I want you to do Stephanie's. Just you, man, no one else. You're my friend, and I just know you'd take good care of her. Steph…she always liked you." "She did?" Norman questioned the last part of Steve's comment. When there was no response to his question he gave his own answer. "Yes, I'll do it, of course." "Good, I'll get the room booked for after your shift, okay?" As Steve exited the room, he paused. "Tomorrow's Friday," Steve just realized. "Sorry man, am I imposing, do you have plans? One of your e-dates, maybe?" Norman shook his head no, afraid if he was to answer he would unwillingly say something he'd regret.

Once his officemate left the room, Norman whispered to himself under his breath. "Do I have plans? Now I do." Kneeling down, he picked up all the pills he spilled, but instead of putting them back into the bottle, he carried them over to the trashcan and disposed of them. He didn't want to numb or repress himself, not now, not anymore. Standing in the middle of the room, Norman allowed his mind to take over his body. Like a computer, his brain processed the multitude of thoughts he was having. Looking through the interior window in his office, the noisy clerk made an observation to her friend. "He's doing it again." "What?" "That thing where he just stands and stares blankly...at God knows what." "My mother stares like that when she's having a seizure. Maybe he's having a seizure." "No, he's just in deep thought. When he snaps out of it he'll have a breakthrough on his work, or a brilliant theory on some scientific mumbo-jumbo the rest of us have no idea about. The Captain always says its best to let him be." "Oh. Okay." "Yeah, well it still creeps me the hell out." The next eight hours went by at a snail's pace. Nothing Norman did passed the time fast enough: lab work, writing reports, not even playing solitaire on his computer helped. Steve had called in some favors with the coroner's office, and two hours were reserved for Norman—3 to 5 a.m. The coroner's lab was the oldest room in an adjoining building connected to the Las Vegas Police Department. Norman hadn't been to this room in some time, and had forgotten just how white and sterile it was. He shivered, swearing that all this colorlessness was adding to the chill he felt. While it must have been 75 degrees outside, it was easily below 40 inside the autopsy room. Locking the door behind him, he approached the snow-white, cloth-draped body. Underneath it he knew, lay Stephanie, the object of his most intimate desires. Had her husband known how he lusted for her, would he have asked him to do this? Would he have given him this perfect opportunity? Norman was positive he wouldn't have. Norman struggled with his decision for the entire day. Dropping his overflowing backpack to the floor, he approached the body slowly, still flipping an imaginary coin in his head. If he was to do this, there would be no going back. Accepting this mantle would tie him eternally into a long family legacy. The closer he stepped to the sheet-draped body, the more it took shape. Those breasts, they were unmistakably hers. Dropping to his knees alongside the table, he took a closer look at her body's profile. "Your body from this angle, it's like a range of snow-topped mountains," he said softly. Panning her covered form from side to side, he once again found himself focused on her breasts. "And your breasts; hills like white elephants," he quoted the title of his favorite Hemingway short story. He liked to think that had Stephanie been alive, she would have found his words a well-said compliment. Perhaps, he thought, she might have even rewarded his niceties with a kiss on the cheek. Standing back up, he retrieved his bag, then dropping the contents on a metal table parallel to the body.

As always, the majority of his bag's encumbrance was books which he stacked carefully atop one another while reading off their titles, marking off the checklist in his head. "This...is both terrifying and exciting, Stephanie. I wish you were here to share this moment with me," Norman chuckled. "Well, I guess in a way you already are. After organizing the jars that were inside his bag into a neat line, he hung his head down, placing his face into his open palms. His mind was a throbbing question mark. There was no clear decision to be had, yet when he looked back at Stephanie, resting peacefully under her blanket, he knew exactly where to uncover this elusive answer. Standing with his hips pressed to the cold metal table, Norman reran the verbal list of things Steve wanted him to check for during the autopsy. So many mysterious ailments could have caused her sudden death and to discover the clues to such would require a full dissection. Running his bare hand over the sheet where her left breast rose up, he felt for her nipple, and when he didn't find it, he yanked the sheet off of her in one fast, violent yank. Gazing down at her nude body, his answer was suddenly obvious. There was no way he would put a scalpel to the beautiful caramel skin of such a striking woman, regardless of her state of death. He would have preferred to get to her sooner, before rigor mortis set in. He looked at his watch, counting the hours from the assumed time of death; with any hopes Stephanie would be in the stages of secondary laxity. Gently wrapping his fingers around her thin wrist, he tugged at her arm, attempting to lift it. He was in luck, her muscles had relaxed. "I hope this works," he whispered. Returning to the table that had his books laid out on it, he retrieved two of the small medical jars he'd lined up. "I've been reading about the dead most of my life. So many different cultures, so many different rituals, and I pieced them all together. I used science to uncover the facts buried like relics in the falsehoods." He talked as he unscrewed the lids on both mayonnaise-sized containers. "The Egyptians practiced this knowledge while the Romans protected it. Nazi Germany sought the secrets, too, but wouldn't you know it, science solved the mystery. It was my grandfather who resurrected Necromancy in the modern day." Inside the two jars were ashes, fresh from a cremation performed this very day. Pouring them out, he covered Stephanie's body neck to toe in the gray and black flakes. "How do I know this will work?" Norman continued his conversation with the dead woman. "I brought a rat back to life two days after it died in a trap, that's how." Picking up the scalpel that was meant to pierce Stephanie's perfect skin, he turned the blade upon himself, cutting open first his left and then his right palm. Holding his hands palm up, he waited for the blood to pool a moment, all the while gritting his teeth through the echoes of pain. Once satisfied with the amount of blood collected in his hands, he turned them around and planted them both on Stephanie's body. Positioning his left hand on her stomach and his right on her heart, he began the second stage of the ritual. Beginning with large circular motions, he massaged his blood and the ash of a dead man into Stephanie's skin. Slowly, the circles tightened as he worked her flesh from top to bottom.

Focused to a degree of tunnel vision, his heart skipped as his right hand brushed over her right breast, his index finger reading her exposed nipple like brail. "Soon, Norman, soon," he tried to calm his building desire. Once her body was coated in ash and blood, he took a step back. There was yet more to be done. Reaching into the pocket of his bag, he produced a metal hip flask and a large roll of gauze. Tipping the flask to her pale, colorless tips, he emptied it until the fluids in the container backed up and spilled down her face. After cutting open the gauze, he bound her wrists tightly together, her hands flat in a prayer gesture of which the irony he didn't miss. Looking at his watch, he saw an hour had passed; he had to hurry. Quickly he tied her ankles with the gauze, then abruptly left the room. Not sixty seconds later, Norman returned with an emergency defibrillator in his hands. Opening the case and pressing the on button began a digital recording that instructed the user how to operate the device, but Norman already knew how it worked. With the electrode patches in place, the device instructed him to make sure everyone was clear of the body. Unable to wait another second, he stepped back and engaged the device. A shock of 200 joules coursed through Stephanie's body, sending a tremor through her limbs. When nothing happened, he pressed the button again, sending a second shock into her. Suddenly, Stephanie's eyes opened. Sitting up at the waist, she looked wildly around the room, her eyes like that of a hunted deer. Trying to speak, only a raspy scratch was heard. Norman snapped his fingers, drawing her attention to him. One final step was required, something his grandfather wrote in his journal. A collection of scrawling words and half sentences that Norman had deciphered the meaning of. This one statement must be said, in order for the master to control the dead; he needed to both consume and be consumed. Still bleeding from the self-inflected wounds on his hands, he pressed his left palm to Stephanie's mouth while bracing her neck with his right. Resisting him at first, he watched as her blonde hair shook, slithering over his hands like hundreds of small snakes, and it was then that he figured what he would consume. Reaching back to the metal stand, he retrieved the scalpel, and with a quick swipe, cut a lock of hair from the back of her head. Still trying to talk, Stephanie struggled to move from the autopsy table. "Stay there." His command had some effect, as she stopped moving and cocked her head to the side like a confused dog. Stuffing her hair into his mouth, he tried to swallow it down, choking at first. Luckily there were still contents in his hip flask. Once he had a mouthful of water, the hair passed much easier down his throat. Was he akin to God? he wondered. No, he hadn't raised the dead, he'd only reanimated it and enslaved it. She was his now, just like the rat, she would follow his every command. Norman hadn't taken his eyes off her breasts since she'd sat up. The way they hung, the implied weight, they were magnificent.

"Can you talk?" Her voice squeaked again. Something was wrong, or maybe not. Her cause of death became more and more apparent. With his thumb and index finger, he spread open her right eyelid, and as he suspected, blood vessels in her eyes had burst, leaving a splattering of red dots on her cornea. "It was an allergic reaction, wasn't it? Your throat closed and you asphyxiated." Stephanie didn't answer. The moving corpse before him was only here in body, not soul. This Stephanie, his Stephanie, had no memories of her life. "Let me try something," Norman whispered as he cut the gauze around her wrists and ankles. Commanding her to stand, he felt a touch of intoxication with the power he had over her. "Stay." Walking a circle around her, Norman witnessed her gaze stay locked on him, no matter where he moved to. When he was behind her, she spun around, and when he was standing behind a pillar, she tilted her head in an effort to see him. A beeping on his watch alerted him to the time. It was 4:30 a.m. and he had scarce time to cover up what he'd done. "In my bag there are clothes for you, and a black wig. Put them all on, now." Stephanie moved slowly at first, but Norman didn't find her stiffness much to be concerned with. Well studied in death, he knew of its many side effects. In addition, his grandfather's journal spoke of this and the solution was simple, all Norman needed to do was warm her up. "Let's hurry! When we get home, I'll make a nice hot bubble bath for you." Norman stood at the threshold between his master bedroom and the master bathroom. Sipping from a glass of wine he'd poured himself fifteen minutes ago, he watched Stephanie bathe. He couldn't believe his luck, for a dead-girl, she looked good. Her body had been found shortly after death and cold-stored at the coroner's office right away. Tracing every line of her body as she scrubbed it with soap in the bubble-filled garden tub, he imagined that this was how happy his officemate Steve must have felt, having such a treasure of a wife. "Finish up in there and come to bed, okay?" "Yes…" her voice squeaked, catching Norman's attention as he left the room. "Yes, what?" "Master." Master. He liked the sound of that, but allegiance wasn't what he sought after this night, it was love. Sitting on the edge of his bed, he awaited Stephanie, his mind still a clutter of uncertainty. Her emerging from the brightly-lit bathroom into the dark bedroom turned her naked body into a black silhouette. She tried to speak, but her scratchy voice wasn't making sense to him. Frustrated, he summoned her closer, so he could both see and hear her better. "Command me," she said. "Do you…" he wanted to say love but didn't have the courage to. "Do you like me?" She nodded yes, her eyes affixed on him. "How do you feel?" This time she answered with a sly smile which Norman took as an indication that she was good to go. Reaching up to her breasts from where he sat, he squeezed them vigorously. After all this time, finally touching them made his heart skip a beat—he was aroused instantly. "You know what I want." He guided her hand to his crotch while looking into her blood-speckled eyes. It was as if placing her hand on his bulge flipped a switch in her head. After tearing off his pants, she pleased him with all the finesse of a coke-whore.

Was this what my grandfather meant when he scribbled in his journal that the dead aren't truly the living? he wondered. Had he made a serious mistake? Was she nothing more than a zombie? His mind wouldn't stop working long enough to enjoy the moment, further calculating every second until an answer was found. He recalled Steve always saying, 'no risk, no reward.' Giving in to Stephanie, Norman shut out his fear, emptied his mind, and laid back to enjoy the first spoils of his labor. Norman didn't make love to her; he wasn't ready yet. But he did lay awake for hours imagining how great it would be. Stephanie didn't sleep, instead she moved about his house, doing what he could only describe as exploring. She was restless, another note his grandfather had scribbled in his journal. The dead don't sleep. He had prepared for this as well. Sitting atop his dresser was a small bottle of Ambien CR, his own prescription. When he found Stephanie that morning, she'd gone through all the food in the kitchen, dry, refrigerated and frozen. A half-eaten plate of raw ground beef was on the kitchen counter, the remainder of which was on the floor where Shelly was finishing it up, the dog enjoying its snack. "Stephanie, I need to go to work, but before I do, I want you to take these pills and get in bed, okay?" "If you wish." Her voice was much improved today. "Tonight we'll go out to dinner." Looking about the room, he guessed what would be best fitting. "How 'bout sushi? Okay?" "Yes, Master." "Our first date," Norman smiled. His smile grew wider; he finally had he wanted. As he drove to work down the busy Oran K. Gragson Highway, he retraced his steps from yesterday. Norman was a thinking man, and in life had learned almost anything was possible with a well-thought-out plan. He had created everything needed to cover his tracks. The morgue always held a John Doe or two, and lucky for him there were three at the moment—two men and a woman. When he arrived at work, he went right to the woman's paperwork in the coroner's office, so he could re-tag her as Stephanie. He left an order for the morning crew to cremate her first thing when they arrived. Convincing Steve would be the hard part. Norman hoped that Steve would already be too distraught to be able to dig deeper into the 'tragic' mistake made by the busy coroner's office. Regardless, he had to fake a few toxicology reports, and write an autopsy description so he had something to show for the time spent last night when he was supposed to be giving Stephanie and autopsy. Child's play, Norman thought to himself. And later that morning, the woman was cremated, his plan working perfectly when everyone thought it was Stephanie instead. Steve left three voicemail messages on Norman's work phone later in the day, and one on his cell. Norman didn't reply to any of them until he had his chance to act the concerned friend, and call the coroner's office himself to demand answers as to how such a mishap could occur. After enough time passed, he returned the calls. "Norman, what the hell happened?" Steve's voice cracked.

"I don't know. The coroner's office just told me she was cremated first thing this morning. Apparently they mixed up the bodies." "Those bastards! They told me the same dammed thing." "It wasn't me, all my paperwork was spot on." "I know, man," Steve's voice lost its anger. "Norman, you're an anal son-of-a-bitch, I knew this couldn't be your mistake." "I'm sorry..." Norman paused. "Do you want to know?" "Know what?" Steve asked. "The results of the autopsy." "What you found? Hell, yes." "Her throat was closed down, and her eyes had burst vessels," Norman said. "My best deduction is she had an allergic reaction. I'm waiting on some blood work, then..." "Thanks, man," Steve began to cry. "I'll let you know, all right?" "Norman, she was so beautiful and sweet. We were going to start a family soon. We were actually trying to conceive while on vacation." Steve's sobbing grew louder and louder to the point where Norman phased him out. Guilt was taking over in his heart. For as happy as he felt this morning when leaving the house, he now felt equally sick and disgusted with himself. "I've got to go, Steve." He hung up the phone abruptly. Norman couldn't stop thinking about Steve's weeping. Steve was the closest thing to a friend he had, and Norman felt like he'd ruined him. Rubbing his temples with the knuckles of his index fingers, he gazed across the office. There was the photo of Stephanie in her bikini, a flickering light in the ceiling directly above, as if it was focused on the picture like a spotlight. He sighed. Using Stephanie like this, he unexpectedly decided, was all wrong. He had time to think on the way home. He would have to kill her, if that was even the right terminology; it was more like disposing of the dead. As he pulled into his driveway, he was astounded to find no lights on in his house; at least the neighbors wouldn't wonder who was in there, sharing the eternal bachelor's residence. "Stephanie?" he called out as he entered his dark home, closing the front door behind him. "Where are you?" There was an overwhelming odor in the house, like rotting garbage. The mess in the kitchen must be worse than he thought. Rounding the hallway to the bedroom, he thought he heard the floor creek. "Stephanie?" He figured there was only one logical thing he could do—burn her. It was the only way to entirely wipe his mistake clean. Flipping the light switch on illuminated his bedroom and the surprise waiting for him. Stephanie must have rummaged through his closet. The pile of clothes on the floor and socks hanging off the dresser and bureau were his first hints to her actions. As he entered the room, Norman heard the shower running. That must be where she is, he thought. If he was to end her, the shower would be an ideal location. Sneaking through the bedroom, careful not to make a sound, he pushed open the door to the master bath, gently and slowly. Steam from the hot water floated stagnantly in the room, fogging up the mirrors and glass doors to the shower. Standing several feet from the double doors of the shower, he hypostasized different ways of ending her unnatural life. He could slide the door open and throw a plastic bag over her head, but he'd noticed last night that she no longer breathed. He considered breaking her neck, he'd seen it done so many times in the movies, and having a firm grasp on human anatomy, he figured he could do it with ease.

It felt like a good plan, but he wasn't convinced it would bring a conclusion to her undead life. While pondering his options, he had a new idea. Electricity. It was one of the elements needed to bring her back, perhaps it would work in the opposite. Norman had stolen the emergency defibrillator he used the previous night. He was afraid it might hold DNA evidence, so he'd brought it home. As he stepped to leave the bathroom, he heard her voice. "Norman?" As much as he wanted to stay silent, he was compelled to speak. "Yes it's me." "I'm so glad your home. Come join me in the shower. The water feels great!" Stephanie slid open the door, revealing herself to him. Her skin, although noticeably paler from yesterday, was tinted red from the hot water. He noticed her tremble as he stared longingly at her breasts, the splotchiest part of her body. Dropping his gaze down to her pelvis, he began to overlook the nagging guilt he'd felt most of the day. "What would you like?" "What?" he asked. "Are you joining me in here, or am I joining you in bed?" He desired her more than anything, but the more he looked at her, the more he saw the married woman from the photograph on Steve's desk. Hearing continuous splashing, he looked down. His shower was backing up again, clogged with her long hair, no doubt. Stephanie was standing in at least three inches of bubbly, soapy water. "Shut the door, I'll be right back," he said. After retrieving an extension cord he kept in his nightstand, he plugged it into the wall and attached his old hair dryer, a model long since recalled for overheating. Why he kept it all these years, he didn't know, but now it would serve one last purpose. Holding a deep breath, he turned on the hair dryer and slid open the shower door, tossing it into the water in the shower stall. That was the easy part; watching Stephanie being electrocuted was much more difficult. She shook from head to toe, her teeth clattering all the while. When Norman heard a popping sound—so eerie and abnormal in its emanation—he dashed over to the electrical outlet and pulled the plug. Crumbling like a ragdoll, Stephanie fell out of the shower to land heavily on the bathroom floor, dead once more. Now all he had to do was burn the body. Four weeks passed before Norman felt like himself again. Steve had been back for a few days, and no one was the wiser as to what Norman had done. He'd made a breakthrough on the big case he was working on and was presenting his findings to Steve to double check, when he noticed that the picture of Stephanie in her bikini was gone from Steve's desk. Suddenly its absence filled the room. Like he was missing his front teeth, Norman felt the awkwardness of it. "Where'd your picture go?" he asked Steve. "Yeah, I know you enjoyed staring at her boobs as much as I did, buddy, but it was time to get rid of it." "Oh, right, sorry." "No worries. It's cool. You don't marry a girl as hot as Steph without taking on the burden of having other men lust after her." "I wouldn't know." "It's not something every man can deal with."

Steve patted Norman on the shoulder after taking the written report from him to study. After work Norman sat at home watching TV. He couldn't stop obsessing over what Steve had said. Was Steve trying to say that Norman wasn't man enough to have a super-attractive girlfriend? Was he mocking him? A local news brief interrupted his scheduled programming. Leah Lavender, a Vegas showgirl, had just been crowned Miss Nevada. Her story was everywhere, the newspaper that sat on his kitchen table, every other internet news site, and tweeted and re-tweeted adnauseam. Norman had followed her rise to fame casually until this very moment, when her image on the TV clicked in his head. Norman couldn't believe how beautiful she was, like a Greek goddess, she stood tall and strong in her bikini during the swimsuit portion of the contest. Those long, tight, shiny legs—he knew the moment he saw her that she was the one, the woman he would spend the rest of his life with. "Oh, it would be so terrible if she had an accident, right, Shelly?" Shelly wagged her tail until Norman stood up, bent over, and patted her on the head. Norman called out of work the following day, so he could prepare. The news brief said Leah would be signing autographs at the Hard Rock from 5-7 p.m. He knew he had to make his move now, while she was easily approachable, because after today, she would be on tour across America. If he really wanted her, he knew he would have to kill Miss Nevada in front of hundreds of people. When he arrived at the signing, the lines were out the door of the hotel. There must have been in excess of five hundred men there, all clamoring over Leah like she was Helen of Troy. As annoying as it was to stand in line for all those hours, it was empowering, too. Every single one of the drooling men proved Norman's case—she was perfect. While in line, security told everyone they had time for two signatures only, no pictures. Norman hoped the Hard Rock was selling 8x10 glossies of Leah to everyone, so they had something for her to sign. This was important for the completion of his master plan. He bought two of them and quickly used them to exact his plan. When he grew closer to the end of the line, all eyes were forward and locked on Leah, giving him ample time to organize himself. No one was paying attention to him, he noted. If he'd wanted to, he could have relieved himself on the carpet or on the slacks of the business suit-wearing metro-sexual standing in front of him, he was that blended into the crowd. "Hi-ya," Leah Lavender chirped as Norman stepped up for his autographs. "What's your name?" "Norman." "To Norman then?" she asked, wanting to know how he wanted the autographs. "Actually, I was hoping you would just autograph them both and maybe kiss the corner where you sign…" Norman paused and smiled, trying his best to be charming. "Like, leave a lipstick mark?" "Gladly!" After each signature, Leah pressed her lips hard against the photo. Norman smiled and politely thanked her before stepping out of line. She had done exactly what he asked, and because of that kindness, she had effectively killed herself. The news of her death filled the airways the following day. Norman would have enjoyed gloating, had he been able to tell anyone at work.

His plan had worked perfectly. Enough of the powder based cyanide he'd smeared on the photos had found its way into her bloodstream from the encounter with her lips. "Hey, Norman, did you hear who's in our cold storage?" Steve called over to him. Norman was nose-deep in paperwork. "Who?" "Leah Lavender, Miss Vegas herself," Steve announced. "She OD'd and now the coroner's office has her. Real shame too. She was hot." "Never seen her," Norman lied, wanting to keep his involvement as low key as possible. "Well, maybe you should go snatch a peek at her while she's fresh." "That's gross." Steve laughed. "Yeah, right, like you with all your dead books never thought of it before." Norman's heart dropped, his muscles seized and his skin went instantly cold. What did Steve mean by that? He was afraid to know. "Thought of what?" Norman repeated. "You know." "What?" "Never mind, buddy." Steve's comments were making him nervous, but not so much that he would alter his plan. Tonight he would raise his new love, Leah Lavender, from the dead. Writing in his grandfather's journal, Norman detailed his process for reanimating Leah's body. He felt obligated to add his information into it also, the only family record he had. Leah's resurrection had gone much smoother than Stephanie's, with the exception of the state of rigor mortis she was in. The electrical jolt of the emergency defibrillator awakened the dormant muscles during the process, he noted in the journal. In order to protect himself and mask her identity as Miss Nevada, Norman had Leah dye her stunning blonde hair black and cut it into a sexy 'bob' hair style. Feeling quite good with himself, he called in sick again. He was going to spend the day with his new girlfriend. "What should we call you?" "Call me?" she asked from the bathroom where she was still trimming her hair. "Your new name?" "Oh, whatever you wish, my love. I'm here because of you. You should pick it." "How about, Elsa?" "I love it!" she cooed with excitement from the bathroom. "Great then. Let's go to bed, tomorrow we go shopping!" Elsa dashed to the bed in the darkness of the room. Norman felt the touch of her bare skin under the sheets; it was ice cold, jarring his senses. Recoiling back as she wrapped her long legs around his body, she could see the rejection in his eyes and Norman sensed her change in mood. "No, Elsa, it's not you. I just wasn't expecting your skin to be so cold," he tried his best to apologize. "I'll just need to warm you up first." "Please warm me up." After taking off his shirt and throwing it to the floor, Elsa ran her cold hand over his hairy chest. "Come here." Norman instructed her to get on top of him. "What do you have in mind?" "Did you swallow all of your pills?" "Of course." "Great, your lack of circulation makes the effects of the drug take longer to commence. Upping the dosage…" Norman stopped speaking, when he saw her eyes flutter. Elsa's head bobbed over his groin as she pulled his underwear down. Something was wrong, and when he realized what it was, it was too late. "Wait, how many pills did you take?" "All of them."

Her forehead landed softly on his lower stomach as she passed out. There must have been twelve pills left in the bottle, if she took them and the four he gave her, she had taken four times the dosage he'd calculated. He was surprised they worked so fast, a good item to note in his grandfather's journal, he thought to himself as he squirmed out from under her. "Good information, but bad timing," he said, adjusting himself through his underwear. The following day went as planned. Elsa finally roused an hour after he did; the Ambien CR had done its job nicely. After a long bath, he escorted her out to the Premium Outlets, an impressive collection of one hundred and fifty stores. It was a beautiful day out, sunny and leveling off at around ninety degrees. A light breeze kept the air moving, and carried the scent of mixed perfumes in the air. Not only did the wealthy housewives and boy toys shop at here, but tourists and traveling celebs alike. After five long hours of shopping, Elsa had turned a thousand heads and Norman felt like a god standing arm and arm with his goddess. "Are you hungry?" he asked her. "I don' know." "Is there anything wrong?" "I guess I'm just tired, and my feet hurt," she replied with a puzzled look on her face. "Then let's go home." As laborious and expensive as shopping was, Norman kept his mind on the prize. When his car came to a rocking stop in his garage, he instructed Elsa to go inside and get ready to begin the private fashion show after she bathed. Pouring himself a glass of wine, he settled into his old leather recliner. A path had been cleared from the bedroom through the living room, a makeshift runway lit by bright lights. He waited, shaking his right leg impatiently. What was taking her so long? he wondered? "Elsa? Hurry it up!" "I…I… okay. Yes, my love." Pushing back, he rested his weight deeper into the chair. This was going to be the best night of his life, he just knew it. The scent of her perfume entered the room a moment before she did. The poor girl must have spilled it on herself, it was that potent, near sickening even. Entering the room atop a pair of six inch high heels, Elsa moved oddly for a woman who had such vast experience with dance. Although her body was decorated by the tightest spaghetti-strapped tube dress he'd ever seen, his attention was drawn down to her best attribute, her legs. The bright light from above washed out her already whitish skin, but not enough to disguise the discoloring that painted her legs from her knees down to her feet. Her once perfect skin was now purple, black and brown, like a deep bruise. Norman's eyes consumed the sight inch by inch; there was something else amiss. He noticed a hobble in her step as she tried to turn before him. Her left ankle was swollen, but her right looked like something on a butcher's block, twisted and rutted. Although he knew exactly what he was looking at, Norman couldn't draw a line between the parallels, connecting them would be admitting defeat. "Elsa, are you…" Norman looked up to her face, admittedly having spent his attention focused the entire time on her body since she'd entered the room. She was still wearing the dark sunglasses he had asked her to adorn when they went out. "Take off the glasses." She did what he asked, and for a moment he wished she hadn't. Elsa eyes had bulged out like a day old corpse.

Faced with this fact, he could no longer deny it, Elsa was still decomposing. "No!" he snapped as he stood. Something was wrong. Had he performed the ritual with error? Had she not been preserved properly before he stole her away? Or was it just his bad luck. For a man of science, he was beginning to believe in the opposite. Luck, karma or fate, whatever word was chosen, it was a cancer invading his life. "Take off your dress." "Gladly my love," she replied, not a drop of modesty in her voice. As she peeled the dress off, Norman noticed the roundness of her belly, although slight, but to a man who searched for clues all day on corpses, it was as clear as day. Elsa was beginning to bloat. He knew the timeline of postmortem changes, and if she was this far along already, even after the ritual, there would be little time before things got worse and much, much more disgusting. "Lea-Elsa, I'm so sorry," he said, shaking his head in disappointment. "Sorry? Why?" After pacing back and forth a few times, Norman said what was on his mind. "This, us, it's not going to work out." "What do you mean?" she asked, walking towards him. "I think we should go our separate ways," Norman answered, turning his back on her. He couldn't look at her any longer, to do so would be to face another failure and he didn't handle failure well. "Have I displeased you, my love?" Elsa gripped his shoulders as she spoke, leaning her head over his right to whisper into his ear. "Yes-no." "Command me. How may I please you…" she whispered until he jerked forward out of her hands. "No! It's over!" Norman stomped five steps ahead before spinning around. He expected to find her standing there looking lost, maybe even sad, but instead she was on his heels as he turned. Tackled hard to the bed, the crown of Norman's head struck the headboard, scrambling his bearings. He swung his arms wildly just like he had when he was a child trying to defend himself from the bullies during recess. His fists found only air until his vision righted itself. She was below him, then to his side, a blur of movement in his watering eyes. "Stop!" he screamed. "You want to abandon me. Why do you want to abandon me?" she screamed. "Get off me!" Norman yelled again when he felt her hands claw down his legs. Wiping his eyes helped return their clarity. She was standing on the bed now, directly above him. Her body quaking, he heard a sloshing sound coming from her stomach a moment before she began to gag. Caught staring like a deer in the headlights of an oncoming car, he looked up at her as she choked like a cat about to throw up a hair ball. As her head lurched forward with a dry heave, Norman snapped out of it. There was no way in hell he wanted to find out that intimately what was about to spill from her digestive system. Grabbing her ankle in both his hands, he twisted until it buckled and she fell backwards. Tumbling over, she disappeared off the end of the bed. "Stop this now! I command you!" Norman yelled as he sprinted from the room. "Run for it, Shelly! Here, girl!" he called to his dog.

Although he didn't look back, he heard Elsa's heeled feet click-clacking behind him. He dashed out the front door, slamming it behind him so quickly that Shelly almost didn't make it through. Norman was an easy thirty steps down the driveway before he looked back, fully fueled by the fear that Elsa was going to be fast upon him, but she wasn't. "Where is she, Shelly?" Norman asked his dog as he looked from side to side. She must still be inside, he concluded a moment before the adrenaline that was holding him up suddenly receded. He flopped to the ground, landing on the cement in an almost Indian-style seat. His mind, like his will to run away, was gone—he had to rest. The sun rose the following morning with Norman still sitting in his driveway. His front yard sprinklers engaged, soaking him a bit before he rose. He had thought about it long and hard. Perhaps the bloodline of Necromancers in his family started and ended with his grandfather after all. After keying in the code to his garage door, he picked up the old, metal gas can that had been his father's. Testing its weight, he could tell it was more than three quarters full as the fuel sloshed within. Popping the cap off, he let it roll across the garage floor; it mattered not where it rested. Splashing the gas against the interior door leading into the house, and around the garage, gave him a freeing sensation. With each gurgle, the metal can released a liter of gasoline and a step closer to his emancipation Norman became. "It all has to burn," he told himself when he realized his grandfather's journal was still inside the house. He encircled his home once before running out of gasoline. He hadn't seen Elsa through the windows or sliding door, but his senses told him she was still inside. In his car was a pack of matches from a bar he'd met a girl at on one of the e-dates. He struck one and watched it burn to his finger tips before throwing it down, then he struck another. "Goodbye, Elsa." Six months had passed with Norman living in a small, pet-friendly apartment. After the night of the fire, he wanted to start over from scratch. His first move was finding a new profession that operated during daylight hours was. It was clear to him that he needed a new job, one that surrounded him with the living, which is why he accepted a job in the science department at Centennial High School. Dr. Norman Mixter was happy to be a teacher. "In today's lesson, we will go over the human skeletal system. Now, who wants to go into the closet and get our old bag of bones out for the class?" Johnny, the biggest troublemaker in the class, raised his hand with a smirk on his face. "Looks like no one else wants to get her, so go ahead, Johnny." "Sweet!" Johnny walked to the back of the classroom as Norman continued to write the lesson plan on the chalkboard. The closet, which was as tall as Johnny, had been reconfigured to hold only one thing—the science department's skeleton. When he opened the door, Johnny screamed with fright, jumped back, and fell over a chair sitting too far out from its matching desk. "It moved! It freakin' moved!" Johnny yelled. The classroom roared with laughter, and some of the other boys teased Johnny for being such a baby. Everyone found it funny, with the exception of Norman. "Don't be afraid of her, Johnny…" he began to say. "I swear it moved." Red-faced, Johnny pointed at it. "Don't worry class, everything's fine." Norman shifted his gaze to the skeleton. "You can't hurt anyone anymore, can you, Elsa?"

Bloody Crazy by Simon Clark Reviewed by Rick Moore

   At first glance this seems like a "28 Days Later" wannabe, until you check the copyright and realize it's a reprint and was written over a decade earlier than Hodges and Boyle's masterpiece. Not that Clark invented the concept of everyone except a handful of survivors becoming insane murderers overnight—I think Romero deserves credit for that one, having first explored the idea with 1973's The Crazies. In "Blood Crazy" it's the adults who go mad, murdering their offspring and any other child they can get their bloody mitts on. This UK based apocalyptic novel is narrated by a teen who crosses the country with his parents relentlessly pursuing him. He joins with a group of kids who have taken over a hotel, and it's there that they remake society. The leaders, as is often the case in tales such as this, are far more monstrous than the zombie-like murderous mums and dads, since they're aware of the heinousness of their actions. While the start of the book (the sudden society meltdown scenario) is the strongest element, the middle, a spin of sorts on Golding's "Lord of the Flies" is no less engaging, and the end, while perhaps a little predictable, still delivers. There's also an interesting theory for the reason all the adults have gone insane, though regrettably this is presented over many pages of exposition, causing the plot to lose momentum right when it should be going full speed, and would have possibly been better if woven into the storyline throughout, rather than presented all at once. Still, it's a great book for teenagers who love apocalyptic horror or just horror in general, due to its narrator being one. Highly recommended for adults, too. Adults be warned, though. Just try to keep your hand off the axe until you've finished reading it. You wouldn't want to get blood on the pages, now would you? Want more movie, books and even a few video games like this one? Try:

MOVIES: The Crazies (73 and 2010 remake), 28 Day/28 Weeks Later, In the Mouth of Madness, Who Can Kill A Child, The Signal, Pontypool, Cronenberg's Shivers and Rabid.

BOOKS: Dead rage and Blood Rage by Anthony Giangregorio, Breathe by Christopher Fowler, Cell by Stephen King, The Fog by James Herbert and Among Madmen by Jim Starlin & Daina Graziunas.

GAMES: Resident Evil 4, Resident Evil 5, The Suffering.

Deathbreed by Tod Tjersland Reviewed by Rick Moore

Movie director Todd Tjersland, perhaps best known as the sick mind behind the "Faces of Gore" documentaries, continues his intent to offend with "Deathbreed," his first novel. But don't go thinking that making you want to barf is the author's sole intention. I've read so much zombie fiction that a lot of the more recent stuff just bores me because it adds nothing new. While this is a classic siege situation, the author creates characters that are so believable it never stops feeling fresh. Like NOTLD, the characters inability to unite and work together becomes their undoing. Instead, what comes to the fore are all their worst traits— particularly in the case of narrator Jimmy Nyberd, the swing shift clerk at the convenience store in which the book is set, and in his racist boss Bryan. Be warned though, this book is not for the easily offended. If you take the most offensive Troma movie you've ever seen, then dial it up to eleven, you will have an idea how far this book goes. After finishing it, I had to wonder if it would have worked so well if a more mainstream approach had been taken. The book would definitely find a larger audience if it were, but I'd have to say no, because the narrator and his motivations felt real, as opposed to the author just trying to be offensive for the sake of it. "Deathbreed" is flat out hilarious throughout, with the jokes and humorous situations grabbing you on page one and never letting up, but the book also delivers some of the best zombie action sequences, extreme gore, and character conflict a fan of this sub-genre could possibly hope for. In the end I was certainly offended by much of the content, particularly when Jimmy had sex with his comatose beloved on her deathbed. But for serious fans of zombie fiction (provided you go in with the caveats before mentioned in mind) I'd say you'd be hard pushed to find anything better currently available.

Sparrow Rock by Nate Kenyon: Reviewed by Rick Moore

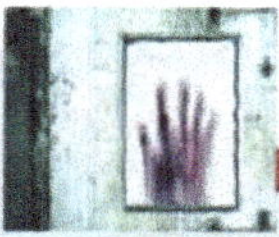

"Sparrow Rock." Not exactly the sort of title that strikes fear into your heart, is it? When a friend pressed the paperback into my hand I was about to ask if it was a novelization of a Jim Henson production, but then I saw the glint in his eyes. This is the glint the guy reserves for special occasions, like the occasion he loaned me "Shock Waves" and I asked him if it was any good, or the time he loaned me his "Deadwood" box set, carefully placing it in my hands and asking me to handle it with the greatest of care. In other words, the glint told me my friend thought "Sparrow Rock' was something a little bit special. After finishing a book, I'll typically look around online to read a few reviews and see if I agree with them. What surprised me, were the number of reviews I found that said the book failed because it just wasn't scary. Now, I read at least one horror title a month, have been for decades, and I have to say this is one of the very few that actually succeeded in giving me that "oh shit" feeling. And that's no easy feat to accomplish. A skilled horror writer can make you experience many emotions, but for me, being a bit long in the tooth, it's pretty unlikely that I'm actually going to feel any kind of palpable sense of fear reading a story. Same for watching most movies, and by scary I don't mean something with a lot of jump-scares (in movies these are the phoniest way to elicit a reaction and film-makers who overuse them should be tarred and feathered as punishment). No, I'm talking about fear achieved by making you experience a mounting sense of dread. Few movies pull this off, and even fewer books. But in "Sparrow Rock," Nate Kenyon succeeds where so many others try, but ultimately fail. The plot of "Sparrow Rock" feels like it's not really going to be a horror novel at all, but instead an apocalyptic thriller. The set up is simple enough: a group of teenagers toting a bag of weed sneak into a bomb shelter built by one of their relatives. No sooner have they blazed up, than the bombs start falling. After surviving for weeks underground, the band of young survivors slowly become aware of a sentient force beyond the safety of the shelter, a force that can't be escaped because the world's already been destroyed, a force that wants inside. "Sparrow Rock" has a set-up that develops into another classic siege scenario, and while the elements that comprise that particular sub-genre are present, what keeps it fresh is the author's skill at ratcheting up the tension. The book moves fast, mainly because plot A involves the end of the world, allowing plot B, the horror plot if you will, to creep to the fore and takeover at the midpoint reveal. As for that reveal, to say too much would ruin the surprise, but suffice it to say that the sense of dread earlier mentioned, is here accomplished by external forces inexorably pushing in and taking over—and to me that's the essence of pure horror.

Freakshow by Bryan Smith: Reviewed by Rick Moore

The protagonists in "Freakshow" begin as interesting, fleshed out people, but as the freaks descend on a small rural town, they come across as little other than pawns to move the plot forwards. As a result, after the first un-put-down-able 100 pages, I felt much less compelled to turn the remainder. Where Smith does succeed is in his bizarro imagery and scenarios—the living car that feeds on people, with its gearstick that becomes a throbbing living vibrator/rape implement takes some topping. What you also get is a touch of "Phantasm" in the origins of the freaks, a touch of steam punk, and bucket loads of exquisitely detailed gore. The book's main weakness is an ending that to me was oddly reminiscent of the revamped "Dr. Who" series, in that the heroes traverse dimensions inside a machine to battle an enormous freak overlord. The outcome, much like in the BBC show, is a given from the moment said overlord's existence is introduced into the narrative. Not as good as Smith's zombie novel "Deathbringer" (it had better characters and less predictable plot developments) but nonetheless an enjoyable read thanks to its weirdness and succession of gory set pieces.

Under the Dome by Stephen King

There have been times over the years where I've struggled through some of King's longer novels, and one occasion where I gave up halfway through because nothing seemed to be happening. I have to admit that when I first picked up the brick that is "Under the Dome," I was very quick to put it down again. That, of course, was before I'd actually opened it. King is often criticized for the length of some of his novels, with reviewers saying they're bloated and that he needs a better editor. Not the case with "Under the Dome." If you're a fan of "The Stand" or "The Mist" you won't be disappointed here. What makes this 1000 plus page novel a must read, is not so much the "Twilight Zone-esque" 'what if' at the heart of the plot, in this case, what if a small town woke to find itself trapped inside a giant invisible dome, but what the characters do to each other as a result of their predicament. There's been a fair bit of talk about the reason for the dome's existence being a let down, and I can see why some reader's feel this way, though personally I had no such qualms. With its numerous characters and plot strands, "Under the Dome" put me in mind of an HBO series, and in Jim Renee the delightfully corrupt councilman who runs the town, King might well be channeling "Deadwood's" Al Swearengen. And who in their right mind wouldn't want to glory in 1000 plus pages of that?

Ideas for great stories are few and far between. Case in point, Stephen King's "The Mist." Don't get me wrong, I love "The Mist" both as novella and film. But isn't "The Mist" basically "Night of the Living Dead" meets Carpenter's "The Fog" topped off with a whole lotta Lovecraft? Yes and no. No because it's the characters the author creates that make his stories so unique, so quintessentially Stephen King. What these people do to each other in the process of dealing with whatever craziness he's dropped them in is why we keep returning to him. Few writers, regardless of genre, have King's skill in creating characters that come so completely alive on the page. So "The Mist" is 100% pure Stephen King, while being at least 50% Romero, Carpenter and Lovecraft. It might be you last read "The Mist" some time in the 80's or 90's, and your most recent visit to that seriously messed-up small town grocery store has only been a journey undertaken with Frank Darabont at the wheel. If that's the case, or if you've never read it, check out the source material of what's easily the last decade's classiest horror film (no small feat for something featuring tentacled monsters).

"The Mist" is King at the absolute top of his game, showing us what a master he is of the long story form. One thing guaranteed to cause heads to be scratched is King's annual top ten film list. 2010 saw the inclusion of "Takers"—hey I love me some Idris Elba too, but c'mon Steve, seriously? In 2009, the universally panned "Last House on the Left" remake made the number 2 slot on King's list, causing cries of "what the hell?" to sound throughout the land. Now, King's love of said remake seems to have crossed over into his writing, since the second novella in "Full Dark, No Stars," titled "Big Driver," details the rape and attempted murder of a female novelist who later undergoes the transformation from victim to would-be vengeance taker. King name checks the Last House remake, saying how much the flick resembles what the novelist has been through, and also gives "The Brave One" a mention, though in fairness, the story, which follows the tried and trusted revenge formula, is handled with King's usual deftness of characterization, and with such quirkiness (the protagonist loses her hold on reality, and councils herself in the voices of her gps and cat) that it never becomes boring, even if the outcome can be guessed from fairly early on. The other novellas in the collection, "1922," "Fair Extension" and "A Good Marriage' find King in fine form. "Fair Extension," the shortest at around forty pages, has a "Needful Things" vibe (a demonic salesman offers a man stricken with cancer a 'fair extension' on life, naturally at a price, and when we discover what is, the story trades its "Twilight Zone" sense of fun, for outright nastiness. "1922" is absolutely stunning for the first 80 pages, then loses some steam, but is still probably my favorite of the four. There are not many writers that have the chops to tell you on page one where the story will be heading for the next sixty pages, in this instance that the protagonist murdered his wife, and still hold you captive as he (the protagonist) recounts every step of the killing, but King pulls it off. He does this on several occasions throughout the book, giving the reader advance knowledge of what's to later occur. Few writers would dare risk such a gambit, but King knows it's the storytelling, not the story alone, and the characters, not just what happens to them, that stand at the foundation of good fiction. "A Good Marriage," gives us some well observed insight into a thirty year marriage, and much of the intimate banality it captures is genuinely touching, but of course this is Stephen King, so when the wife discovers her husband's long held secret, the reveal is anything but banal.

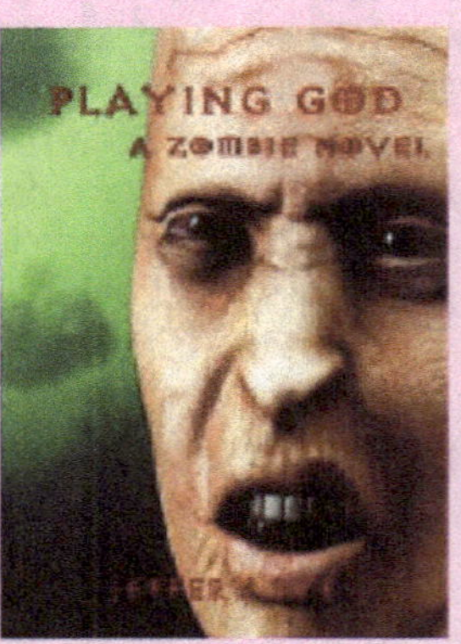

TWITTER OF THE DEAD

By Alan Spencer

RONNYJ> What would your last words be on the way out of this stinking world?
@DAdiego> Are you in trouble? Where are you? Maybe I can help.
RONNYJ> Sioux City. I've been bitten, and I'm blowing this city and every dead thing up and walking off the face of the Earth in 3 city blocks of me.
@DAdiego> Can't help you. I'm in Cincinnati. God be with you.
@radradster> You've been drinking again, or something? Bourbon? Whiskey Creek? What's your poison tonight?
@julieCHINESE> He ain't blowing up anything, save his own dick.
mizzymouse#3> What're going to blow Sioux City up with? Some Roman candles and a canister of gasoline?
projectmanagerchaos12> Throw some nails in the gas canister. It'll be like a grenade from Home Depot.
@ChicagoPDsurvivor> Adios Sioux City! Gawd-damn! Wah-hoo!
mizzymouse#3> Blow us all out of the water, while you're at it. Save me a lifetime of sleeping with one eye open.
@mariaK> Sioux City, huh? Everybody's dead there, except for you, pal. Go ahead and light it up. GOOD-BYE.
RONNYJ> Last words. I'm serious. I've been bitten. Anybody have good suggestions? I'm standing on top of city hall with the control mechanism in my hand.
RONNYJ> One touch of the red button, and 16 squares miles goes up in ash.
RONNYJ> Me and 300 deadheads go up in vapor. I've counted them. I've been up here so long.
@dixter83_mama> How about 'See you in Hell.' Not very original. Best I've got.

@hootieowl90> Die again, and this time don't come back!
mizzymouse#3> I'll shoot you in the head—in Hell! Cheesy, I know.
RadRay> Tell 'em Ray sent ya!
@mariaK> Go with Jesus!
@dixter83_mama> I'd piss off the edge of the roof first, before I said a single word. Hit one right on the head. Right between the eyes. Yellow rain.
RadRay> Sit on it! STINKFACES!
@dixter83_mama> Suck on this meat!
@PEOPLEchallenged> I'm a drifter with a stolen iPhone. The most philosophical thing I've said is, "You've got any change?"
@hootieowl90> Don't be a limp wrist about it. Say something about your cock and balls and engage the switch.
@DAdiego> You sure you're bitten? I knew someone who was mistaken about that, and they shot themselves in the head, thinking they were.
@DAdiego> It was a terrible shame.
@PEOPLEchallenged> He'd be sure, and that other dude's a dumbass. He's lighting us all up. Toasty! Go for it, RONNYJ!
RONNYJ> Yes, I'm certain I'm bitten. The bastard got me on the ear, he took the whole ear. Ear drum's full of blood. Heard him crunching on cartilage before I bashed his brains out with a shovel.
RONNYJ> Any more suggestions before I'm gone? No bullshit. I'm only sticking around for a few more minutes.
@SAFEsammy> I'm in a New York studio apartment. Could care less about Sioux City. Annex it off the map like the rest of the world. Except my apt.
@HelenZebraTime> Canada rules! Give it a month and we'll be zombie free! And still have health care. Bozos!
@hootieowl90> We're going to Hell together! It's all about the emphasis on the right words. I'm saying that when I'm inches from the grave.
@dixter83_mama> Choke on 'em! The mailman said that. Or was it another guy? I can't remember.
@DAdiego> I'd cross myself and push the button. Don't say a word. Show them who's tough and who's dead.
@BUSYBONES> I'll be joining you soon, buddy. One of those damn things took off my ring finger.
@Tiff_tiff> The birds are tweating in my panties.
@pootiesunshine> Shut up, Tiffany. You're a whore. The poor guy's dying, and you're talking about your vagina.
@HelenZebraTime> Tequila sunrise, bitches!
@DAdiego> Thus to tyrants!

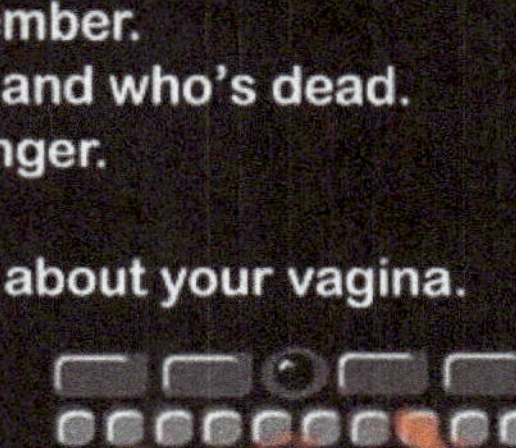

@nastymanBIG> You ever screw a zombie? I'd go out screwing one. I'd cut the head off first.
RadRay> Nasty!

TWITTER OF THE DEAD

@BUSYBONES> COOL IDEA!

@dixter83_mama> 'Fuck all of you sickos.' Those would be my last words after I find these dirty perverts and treat them like they were zombies.

@dixter83_mama> Bullet RIGHT between the eyes, but first I'd shoot their dicks off!

@mizzymouse> First drink's on me, wherever we're all going.

@Tiff_tiff> Suck my poots-eye!

@BUSYBONES> Suck my pussy? Is that what you mean?

@BUSYBONES> Suck my dick more like it.

@DAdiego> God love us all.

RONNYJ> I wish you a better fate than mine. May we all wake up in a better place! GOODBYE.

@DAdiego> Did he do it?

@dixter83> Nah.

@local_CAL> I know that guy. He's a boozer. Sucked the sauce while mopping the floors of an elementary school.

@CalmJones> Nope. I heard what he said, actually. He blew up two blocks. It's all on fire. He must've had TNT or C-4.

@DAdiego> Then he's really dead.

@dixter83_mama> I want to know what he said!

@BUSYBONES> Why? You plan to copy RONNYJ?

@dixter83_mama> Seriously, CalmJones, what did he say?

@dixter83_mama> What'd he say?

@dixter83_mama> Ah, forget it. There's more of those things banging on my door. 12 gauge or 30—.06? What do you think, everyone?

By Adam P. Lewis

UNDEAD TWEETS

WifeyMifey> We had a close call. Zombies broke through the board-up windows. Glen shot three dead. We're okay, just shaken up. about 2 hours ago via Mobile Web

WifeyMifey> Glen taut me how to fire a pistol. I'm covering him as he broads the windows in case he's attacked. He's says I'm a deadeye! about 2 hours ago via Mobile Web

giantrobot454> LOL, U don't need a safe zone. Sounds like you're the new Annie Oakley! Good to hear you and Glen are safe. about 2 hours ago via Twitter for iPhone

WifeyMifey> That I am! ;) Good to hear you're safe too! about 2 hours ago via Mobile Web

ZombieDotGov> Important message #NewYork #Safezone now open in Adirondack State Park west of Lake George on Prospect Mountain with 5,000 available tents. about 2 hours ago via Web
Retweeted by giantrobot454

giantrobot454> I'm heading for the Prospect Mountain safezone. DM me if U want to hitch a ride. I leave in 1 hour. about 2 hours ago via Twitter for iPhone

WifeyMifey> Glen and I R packing light. We've decided to head out w/ a friend to the Prospect Mountain safezone. We leave in 1 hour. Wish us luck!
about 2 hours ago via Mobile Web

WifeyMifey> Glen isn't feeling well. I think he's coming down w/the flu. He has a fever. We'll never be let in the safe zone if he's sick. about 90 minutes ago via Mobile Web

WifeyMifey> The zombies are back. They're pounding on windows and doors. Glen is firing his pistol thru the planks on the windows. about 80 minutes ago via Mobile Web

WifeyMifey> I don't hear the zombies outside the house anymore. I think Glen scared them off. I'd never make it thru this plague of zombies w/out him. about 70 minutes ago via Mobile Web

WifeyMifey> Glenstweets- Thank you for protecting me. I luv U. about 65 minutes ago via Mobile Web

WifeyMifey> Glen collapsed a few minutes ago. He's standing now. He hasn't slept much in the past month. The stress and flu are getting to him. about 1 hour ago via Mobile Web

WifeyMifey> Glen doesn't have the flu. He was bitten on the leg when zombies attacked. He kept it from me. He didn't want to scare me. about 1 hour ago via Mobile Web

WifeyMifey> Glen blacked out. He's weak, cold, and clammy. Anyone know of a #cure? about 1 hour ago via Mobile Web

TWITTER OF THE DEAD

giantrobot454> There's a Dr in Saratoga. He's tweeted he knows a cure for a price. It's a 50 min drive. Think Glen will hold on long enough? about 1 hour ago via Twitter for iPhone

WifeyMifey> giantrobot454. I don't know. He's breathing. But he can't stand. He can't speak. His eyes are glassed over. about 1 hour ago via Mobile Web

giantrobot454> Check his pulse. If you feel one there is time. If he's breathing w/out a pulse then I'm sorry to say there's no hope for him. about 1 hour ago via Twitter for iPhone

WifeyMifey> He has no pulse. His breathing is laboring. I don't want him to turn. Someone #help!
about 1 hour ago via Mobile Web

giantrobot454> He's turning. There's only 1 solution. He taught you how to use a pistol. You have to use it.
50 minutes ago via Twitter for iPhone

WifeyMifey> I understand what I've got to do. It's gonna be tough. He's still my husband no matter what he'll become. 47 minutes ago via Mobile Web

giantrobot454> I'll be here for U if you need me. You'll need peace to come to terms to do what you've got to do. I'll leave you be. 45 minutes ago via Twitter for iPhone

WifeyMifey> 20 years ago I said "I do." 5 minutes ago I said my peace. 38 minutes ago via Mobile Web

WifeyMifey> We're supposed to grow old together and to go RVing around the country. I never planned on ending our marriage with a gun to your head. 35 minutes ago via Mobile Web

WifeyMifey> I've pulled the plug on my mother when breast cancer won. Pulling the trigger and killing my husband is harder. I've lowered the gun twice. 30 minutes ago via Mobile Web

WifeyMifey> What I'm about to do is 'cause I luv U. Thankyou for loving me. Thank you for all the good and bad times. I loved sharing my life with U. 28 minutes ago via Mobile Web

WifeyMifey> Glenstweets I'm sorry. 25 minutes ago via Mobile Web

WifeyMifey> It's done. Glen is dead. 22 minutes ago via Mobile Web

WifeyMifey> I can't stop crying. 15 minutes ago via Mobile Web

WifeyMifey> The gun is still shaking in my hands. 11 minutes ago via Mobile Web

WifeyMifey> If you learn anything from me, it's to hold onto your dreams. My dreams are over. Like mother's cancer, the zombies won. 7 minutes ago via Mobile Web

WifeyMifey> I'm turning the gun on myself. Sorry. 3 minutes ago via Mobile Web

giantrobot454> Peace be with you both. #Godspeed! 1 minute ago via web in reply to WifeyMifey

By Grant Wamack

GHOUL TWEETS

Tany101> I hate watching the news. I think it's a waste of time. They never have anything positive to say.

Tanya101> My husband, John, came back home today with a nasty bite on his leg. Syas he was attacked by some bum. Hope he feels better.

Tanya101> It's getting worse. The bite is definitely infected.

Tanya101> Today took John to the doctor, who dry heaved when she saw his infection.

Tanya101> The neighbors died in their sleep yesterday. They were such a sweet old couple. How sad…

Tanya101> John has been taking the antibiotics the doctor gave him. But they don't seem to be working.

Tanya101> Debating on whether or not I should attend the funeral. Feeling depressed lately.

Tanya101> A fight broke out at the grocery store. One guy bit another man's nose clean off his face. One word: Horrific

Tanya101> Grey skies. Haven't seen the sun in days. Praying it comes out soon and things change for the better.

Tanya101> John's sick in bed. Just lays there and moans all day. Poor baby.

Tanya101> John won't go to the doctor. Why does he have to be so stubborn?

Tanya101> I managed to get a house doctor to come look at John. When he saw John's leg he gasped, mumbled sorry, and left as fast as he could.

Tanya101> I don't know what I'm supposed to do. The hospitals are getting full of sick people and John just lays there all damn day.

Tanya101> Went to the funeral. A little girl bit the priest's neck and ripped out his trachea. What the fuck is going on?

TWITTER OF THE DEAD

Tanya101> I bought a gun today. A small 9mm. It's sleek and easy to handle. I need it for protection. People are starting to act nuts.

Tanya101> John died last night. I'm not quite sure what happened. One minute he was there, holding me in his arms, the next he was gone.

Tanya101> It's a miracle. John came back. I know it sounds crazy, but he just woke up as if nothing happened.

Tanya101> John's been acting strange…a lot more violent.

Tanya101> He bit me. The bastard actually bit me! My own husband.

Tanya101> I just murdered my husband. The love of my life. My hands are covered in his blood. It's getting all over the keyboard!

Tanya101> The bite is getting infected. I'm scared out my mind.

Tanya101> The power's been going on and off and people have been banging on the front door at random times of the day.

Tanya101> A group of 'them' broke in last night. I managed to kill off a couple, but the others…they just kept coming despite being shot.

Tanya101> I've barricaded myself in my home office. I pray to whoever's listening that they don't get in.

Tanya101> I'm getting hungry and thirsty, and they're still here. I hear them moaning at night. It's as if they're in pain.

Tanya101> The infection is getting out of control. My arm looks real bad. I think it's beginning to turn gangrenous :(

Tanya101> I'm beginning to hallucinate. I looked out the window and saw a man getting ripped apart. What remained of him came back to life.

Tanya101> I couldn't stand it anymore. I found a saw in the cellar and managed to cut my own arm off. I rather die than turn into one of them. God, it's painful.

Tanya101> If you're reading this, I'm probably dead or dying. I feel so dizzy and the blood loss is ridiculous. Oceans of red flow out of me.

Tanya101> dljsdisidojaadiojfiooooooooooooooooooooo

TWITTER DEAD

By Joe Filippone

9:30AM From @Hollyweird_Kidd> Dang! Twitter is blowin' up! What's w/ all the zombie stuff? Is it National Zombie Day or something? LOL

10:00AM From @Hollyweird_Kidd> Okay HAHA. Very funny. Zombies are here and eating people. *shudders* Scary. LOL

10:30AM From @Hollyweird_Kidd> Ok it was funny the first few times, now it's effin' old! I'm tired of getting all these tweets from people saying they're being attacked. Jokes over!

11:25AM From @Hollyweird_Kidd> Seriously people—zombies? Is this a publicity stunt for a zombie movie? Oh, I have audition for that Monday! Anyway, Halloween was over a month ago. Let's focus on Xmas.

11:45AM From @Hollyweird_Kidd> Twitter's dead

1:55PM From @Hollyweird_Kidd> Breaking news. New York is gone? WTF is going on!?

2:00PM From @Hollyweird_Kidd> Can't get hold of my parents. Anyone in Denver, Co please contact them. #800-555-9989 Adis 219 W 39th Place Wheat Ridge 55533 Thanks

2:30PM From @Hollyweird_Kidd> Has anyone been able to reach my parents?

3:33PM From @Hollyweird_Kidd> So…I'm guessing that's a no

4:15PM From @Hollyweird_Kidd> Just heard a scream outside. Spooky.

4:45PM From @Hollyweird_Kidd> Damn. Looks like some drunks are hanging out in the alley outside my place. I can see 'em from my window. They're really smashed. They can't even walk straight. Their clothes are torn to shit. Bet they effin' reek.

5:30PM From @Hollyweird_Kidd> Screams everywhere. Been seeing weird things outside. Getting scared

6:00PM From @Hollyweird_Kidd> Anyone there? Want to hang out? Don't wanna be alone. More of those creepy homeless people are hanging around outside.

6:30PM From @Hollyweird_Kidd> Hello? Anyone? Please.

TWITTER OF THE DEAD

7:00PM From @Hollyweird_Kidd> Wish my roommates would get back. Don't like being here alone. Alley is now overrun w/ homeless people. Looks like every degenerate in Hollywood is outside my apt.
830PM From @Hollyweird_Kidd> Still dead on here. Facebook's dead too. Feel like I'm the only one left on Earth.....
9:01PM From @Hollyweird_Kidd> Lost power. Cell phone dying. Roommates still gone. Too quiet in the neighborhood......
9:01PM From @Hollyweird_Kidd> Anyone around?
9:02PM From @Hollyweird_Kidd>Something is trying to break into my apartment!!!! HELP ME!!!!
9:03PM From @Hollyweird_Kidd> PLEASE! NOT JOKING! HELP!
9:04PM From @Hollyweird_Kidd>Is anyone still using Twitter?
9:05PM From @Hollyweird_Kidd> Is anyone else alive? Please. Help me! They're almost in!
9:07PM From @Hollyweird_Kidd> WTF!? No answer at police station. Phone almost dead......SHIT!!!!
9:10PM From @Hollyweird_Kidd>They're in! Hiding in closet! Please. If anyone in Hollywood's reading this...HELP! Addy 9810 Rus

By Joshua Ramey-Renk

>rameyrenk got up this AM late! Anybody still @Starbucks get me a latte Thx
>@rameyrenk umm...no peppermint, thanks, just a latte
>trains late ALREADY & dude w/cold kept hacking on my shoulder #useahanky...ick
>R u all slacking 2day? Half the team out sick DM me if there's a party
>seriously...to the guy puking in the middle of the sidewalk #that's gross
>my client just cancelled my meeting. Anybody in town want to do lunch? DM me
>OMFG I just saw some crazy junkie jump a little old lady #hope she's had her shots
>wtf? Delivery guy just fainted in the lobby and started having seizures #epilepsy
 >#weird day finally going home & trains delayed to the point of cancelled #running late #am walking
>rapid trans need to get their $h¥T together, a bunch homeless sleeping around the station, they look pretty sick too
>some guy who looks like he was in fight keeps staring at me #all bloody #that's weird
 >bloody guy gone, but sidewalks filled with people who look the same. Did I miss a riot?
>anybody else seeing weird people or is it just downtown?
>ok, getting freaked out. I swear I just saw a sleeping homeless guy dragged into an alley
>DO NOT COME DOWNTOWN SOME SERIOUSLY WEIRD CR*P GOIN DOWN
>JUST GOT FOLLOWED for 3 blocks by some kind of gang. They look pretty busted up #taking a cab
>only got two blocks and cab ran over some guy who tried to climb on the hood. Riot??
>WTF is going on? Where is the riot squad? People are starting to get into fights
>ok ok ok. Somebody please tweet back...I think something really bad is going down need cops
>just saw a cop. He was beating some kid
>omfg...that cop just started biting that kid...I think he's got rabies or something
>holy shizzit...the kid must be ok, he just stood up.
>F-this! I'm just going to get inside the tallest building I can. DM or tweet me and send a friggin helicopter or something
>Hey, I can see my office from up here!
>This riot or whatever is huge! Every street I see from up here is packed, lots of burning cars
>that kid followed me onto the roof. Lurching around. Concussion? I'll see if he's ok.
>I think that kid must have been high...he just walked off the friggin edge of the building :(
>I can hear helicopters. Somebody out there tell them there's a guy on the roof of the Rourke Building
>Just got video of helicopter firing something at the riot, or whatever the hell it is. Cannot WAIT to upload it 2nite.
>@rameyrenk because I have a cheap boss and not enough bandwidth on my cell plan to upload it now #duh
>Whoa! Helicopter just flew right passed me, totally ignored me waving and jumping around.
>Must be rescuing people, saw somebody actually clinging to the skids
>IT CRASHED IT CRASHED HOLY SHIZZIT!!! #fireball

TWITTER OF THE DEAD

>FINALLY got somebody's attention, I can hear footsteps in the stairwell. Slow footsteps #careful
>It's the cop who was beating that kid, the rabies dude! He didn't see me.
>Hiding, for frick's sake tell somebody I'm up here alone with a rogue rabies cop!
>he's carrying an arm. A FRIGGIN ARM. I'm stuck hiding in a utility closet. I can hear him out there.
>send help to the top of the Rourke building RETWEET THIS!!!!!
>please send help
>please se
>xzlj6jsjslmscja;sjg;snhosjhoujpmhiomjpiogosmwimhjoanhipimjomjpiohgcjwohpo[JFADILGRGN A;
QCMMJI6YU2 0[[G2

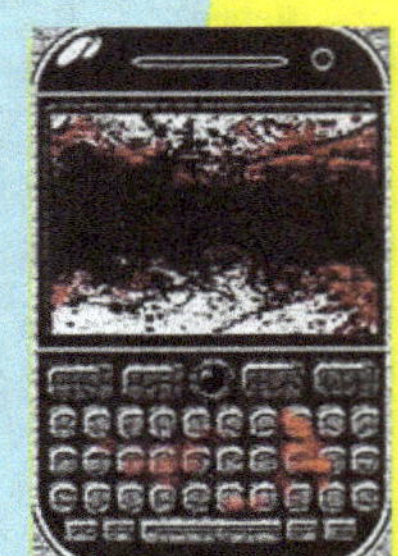

By Kelly Hashway

AliciaSeesAll> Zombies are everywhere! They're hunting people down. about 2 hours ago via Mobile Web
ErikMoss> OMG! They just dragged my neighbor out of his house and they're—OMG! They're tearing him apart.
about 1 hour ago via Mobile Web
MandyB> I can hear their footsteps in the hall outside my apartment. Please, someone help me!
about 1 hour ago via Mobile Web
TrevMan> I'm going to sneak down the fire escape. Anyone else who can get out, meet me at Starbucks. We'll come
up with a plan together. about 45 minutes ago via Mobile Web
AliciaSeesAll> Don't go! It's too dangerous. Hide. Find somewhere they won't look. about 44 minutes ago via
Mobile Web
TrevMan> No way! They'll find me. They can smell flesh a mile away. about 43 minutes ago via Mobile Web
MandyB> They're breaking down my door! Oh God! Someone help me! about 43 minutes ago via Mobile Web
TrevMan> Get the hell out of there! Climb down the fire escape and meet me at Starbucks. GO!
about 40 minutes ago via Mobile Web
ErikMoss> Oh man! They're eating my neighbor. Fighting over who gets the heart. I'm going to be sick.
about 39 minutes ago via Mobile Web
TrevMan> Just be thankful it's not YOUR heart they're fighting over! about 39 minutes ago via Mobile Web
MandyB> I'm going down the fire escape. They're in my apartment now. I couldn't stay there. I'll meet you at
Starbucks. about 38 minutes ago via Mobile Web
AliciaSeesAll> No! Don't go down the fire escape. I can see you from my window. There's a zombie right below you.
Don't move! about 38 minutes ago via Mobile Web
MandyB> Holy crap! What do I do? about 35 minutes ago via Mobile Web
AliciaSeesAll> MandyB Stay still and don't make any noise. about 32 minutes ago via Mobile Web
ErikMoss> I threw up in my garbage can. I only left the window for a minute. The zombies are gone. I don't know
where they are! about 28 minutes ago via Mobile Web
TrevMan> I'm almost to Starbucks. Zombies are everywhere. They're feeding like crazy! about 22 minutes ago
via Mobile Web
ErikMoss> OMG! I found the zombies. They're breaking into my house! about 22 minutes ago via Mobile Web
TrevMan> The hospital is an all you can eat buffet! about 18 minutes ago via Mobile Web
AliciaSeesAll> ErikMoss. Go down to the basement and hide! about 17 minutes ago via Mobile Web
AliciaSeesAll> MandyB. Are you still there? about 15 minutes ago via Mobile Web
MandyB> The zombie is climbing the fire escape! about 15 minutes ago via Mobile Web
TrevMan> MandyB! Find a weapon! Fight! about 14 minutes ago via Mobile Web
MandyB> I'm climbing back up! about 13 minutes ago via Mobile Web
TrevMan> MandyB. Stop tweeting and climb faster! about 13 minutes ago via Mobile Web
AliciaSeesAll> MandyB Let us know when you're back in your apartment. about 12 minutes ago via Mobile Web
ErikMoss> I'm in the basement. Reception down here sucks! Hiding in the gardening tool cabinet.
about 10 minutes ago via Mobile Web
TrevMan> Gardening tools can make good weapons if they find you. about 10 minutes ago via Mobile Web
AliciaSeesAll> MandyB Are you okay? about 9 minutes ago via Mobile Web
ErikMoss> OMG! They're going to find me, aren't they? about 9 minutes ago via Mobile Web

TWITTER OF THE DEAD

TrevMan> AliciaSeesAll Where are you? Are there zombies near you? about 8 minutes ago via Mobile Web
AliciaSeesAll> I'm in an abandoned paint store. No zombies around. Yet. about 8 minutes ago via Mobile Web
TrevMan> New plan. Forget Starbucks. It's swarming with zombies. about 7 minutes ago via Mobile Web
AliciaSeesAll> I'm heading to you. about 6 minutes ago via Mobile Web
AliciaSeesAll> MandyB Please tell us you're okay! about 6 minutes ago via Mobile Web
ErikMoss> They're coming down the stairs. I hear them. How do you kill a zombie with a gardening hoe? about 6 minutes ago via Mobile Web
TrevMan> Oh man! I almost walked right into one of them! It went for an old lady instead though. It was awful but I'm safe. For now. about 5 minutes ago via Mobile Web
AliciaSeesAll> No one is safe! We are all going to die! about 5 minutes ago via Mobile Web
AliciaSeesAll > MandyB Where are you? about 4 minutes ago via Mobile Web
ErikMoss> They're outside the cabinet! about 4 minutes ago via Mobile Web
TrevMan> ErikMoss Fight them man! Hoe their zombie heads off! about 4 minutes ago via Mobile Web
AliciaSeesAll> TrevMan I see you! about 3 minutes ago via Mobile Web
TrevMan> All I'm going to make a run for it. Open the door for me! about 3 minutes ago via Mobile Web
AliciaSeesAll> ErikMoss Are you okay? about 3 minutes ago via Mobile Web
AliciaSeesAll> MandyB Are you there? about 3 minutes ago via Mobile Web
AliciaSeesAll> The door's open. about 2 minutes ago via Mobile Web
AliciaSeesAll> TrevMan Run! They're right behind you! They see you! about 2 minutes ago via Mobile Web
AliciaSeesAll> Is anyone out there? Oh, God! I just saw them kill @TrevMan. about 2 minutes ago via Mobile Web
AliciaSeesAll> Please! Someone. Anyone. Help me! They're coming this way! about 2 minutes ago via Mobile Web
AliciaSeesAll> They're in the store with me! Oh my God! I'm going to die! about 1 minutes ago via Mobile Web

By Kiernan Kelly

QtrbackStar> Went to Holly's funeral yesterday. Back in class now. Bummer. about 60 minutes ago
RagingCajun @QtrbackStar> OMG! Your gf? How'd she die? about 59 minutes ago
QtrbackStar @RagingCajun> Freak pyramid accident. Broke her neck. about 57 minutes ago
RagingCajun @QtrbackStar >Wtf? Why r u in school? Cold, dude. about 56 minutes ago
QtrbackStar @RagingCajun> Bite me. Have practice this afternoon. about 55 minutes ago
RagingCajun @QtrbackStar> Kewl. Bros before hoes. about 54 minutes ago
QtrbackStar @RagingCajun> Truth. L8R. about 53 minutes ago
QtrbackStar>Whoa. Storm came up out of nowhere. Wicked lightning. If we lose power, Coach will call off practice. Sux. about 45 minutes ago
QtrbackStar Lost power. Practice cancelled. Stupid school on lockdown. Don't know why. Nobody's talking here. about 35 minutes ago
RagingCajun @QtrbackStar> Here, too. Heard it was terrorists. Dropped a bomb or something. about 34 minutes ago
QtrbackStar @RagingCajun> Where'd it happen? about 33 minutes ago
RagingCajun @QtrbackStar> IDK, but it sounds bad. about 32 minutes ago
QtrbackStar> People r climbing over da school fence. Nobody's supposed 2 get in during lockdown. Don't know what's up. Some teachers went outside 2 see. about 29 minutes ago
QtrbackStar> Teacher didn't come back. Some of da guys r leaving. Don't know if I want 2 go out there. What if there's radiation or something? about 20 minutes ago
RagingCajun @QtrbackStar> Don't leave. Dude, something's really wrong out there. Like FUBAR wrong. about 19 minutes ago
QtrbackStar> OMFG! Just saw Coach outside da window. He looks hurt. There's so much blood! Wtf is going on? about 15 minutes ago
QtrbackStar @RagingCajun U there? Those people. I swear I'm not crazy, but I think they're dead. Like zombies or something. TMB. about 13 minutes ago